향기로운 우물 이야기

도서출판 아시아에서는 《바이링궐 에디션 한국 대표 소설》을 기획하여 한국의 우수한 문학을 주제별로 엄선해 국내외 독자들에게 소개합니다. 이 기획은 국내외 우수한 번역가들이 참여하여 원작의 품격을 최대한 살렸습니다. 문학을 통해 아시아의 정체성과 가치를 살피는 데 주력해 온 도서출판 아시아는 한국인의 삶을 넓고 깊게 이해하는 데 이 기획이 기여하기를 기대합니다.

Asia Publishers presents some of the very best modern Korean literature to readers worldwide through its new Korean literature series 〈Bilingual Edition Modern Korean Literature〉. We are proud and happy to offer it in the most authoritative translation by renowned translators of Korean literature. We hope that this series helps to build solid bridges between citizens of the world and Koreans through a rich in-depth understanding of Korea.

바이링궐 에디션 한국 대표 소설 038
Bi-lingual Edition Modern Korean Literature 038

The Fragrant Well

박범신
향기로운 우물 이야기

Park Bum-shin

ASIA
PUBLISHERS

Contents

향기로운 우물 이야기

The Fragrant Well

모두들…… 나를 보고 계시군요.

재판이 진행되는 사이사이, 다른 사람이 심문받고 있는 동안에도 무심한 척, 안 보는 척, 힐끗힐끗, 나를 쳐다보는 여러분의 시선을 충분히 느꼈는데요, 이제 맘 놓고 쳐다봐도 되니까 편하시겠어요들.

나의 어디를 보시나요?

눈을 영혼의 창이라고 하던데요. 설마 진실을 알고자 내 영혼의 창을 수시로 훔쳐보는 건 아니실 테구요. 시골 여자치고 반반하네 뭐. 아까 재판정에 들어설 때 어떤 분이 이렇게 속삭이는 걸 들었어요. 아따, 반반하니까 그짓 하다가 감옥 가지. 다른 분의 대꾸가 그쯤 됐으

You're all... looking at me, I see.

All throughout this trial, all while they questioned the others, I felt you stealing your little glances at me, pretending to be uninterested, pretending not to look. How nice for you now that you can just sit back and stare.

Which part of me are you looking at, anyway?

They say the eyes are the windows to the soul, but somehow I doubt you're straining like that to try and catch a glimpse through my windows. Easy on the eyes for a country girl. That's what I heard someone whisper earlier as I entered the court-room. Hell, being easy on the eyes is how she did what she did, why she's going to jail. It's not hard

리라고 상상하는 건 어려운 일이 아니에요. 그러믄요. 여러분이 어떤 상상을 하면서, 나를, 내 몸을 보고 있는지 압니다. 알구말구요. 나도 그랬거든요. 학교 때 친구가 남몰래 남편 아닌 어떤 남자와 여관방에 드나드는 것을 알았을 때, 내 눈도 부지불식간에 그 친구 몸의 구석구석을 훑고 있었으니깐요. 간통이란 말만 들어도 진저리가 쳐졌어요. 공연히 침을 뱉고 싶은, 그러면서도 은밀하게 이끌리는 추악한 호기심이 깃들여져 있어요. 간통이란 말엔. 세상이 달라져서 사람들이 밥 먹듯 간통을 해도 그 말에 깃들여진 관습은 달라지지 않아요. 들키면 간통이고 안 들키면 사랑이죠. 재판장님 눈에도 내가 특별히 화냥기 많은 여자로 보이나요?

죄송해요, 재판장님.

알겠습니다. 방청하는 분들께 일부러 불쾌감을 드릴 생각은 추호도 없어요. 사실은 암말도 안 하고 싶었답니다. 심문받을 때에도 제일 괴로웠던 건 질문 내용이 아니라 말을 해야 한다는 것이었어요. 예, 아니오라고만 대답하시오, 라고 말씀하셨지요? 나는 차라리 계속 입을 다문 채 있고 싶었어요. 예, 아니오, 그게 얼마나 긴 문장이라구요. 공주교도소 앞에 있었던 게 사실입니

to imagine that being someone else's reply, that or something like that, anyway. I know the things you're imagining as you sit there looking at me, at my body. Of course I know. I've done the same thing. When I found out an old school friend of mine was stepping out on her husband, that she'd been in and out of motels with another man, well, that same second my eyes scanned up and down her body, too, looked at all the nooks and crannies. Just the word—adultery—gave me shivers. It pulls you in, makes you feel a furtive, dirty curiosity even as you also want to spit on the whole thing: adultery. It doesn't matter that the world has changed, that people commit adultery now the same way they eat three meals a day: the word still triggers all the same feelings. If you're caught, it's adultery; if you're not, it's love. Do I look like a particularly loose woman to you, too, Your Honor?

I'm sorry, Your Honor.

I understand. I don't have the slightest desire to make things unpleasant for the spectators here. To be honest, I didn't want to say anything at all. That was the hardest part of my interrogation, too; it wasn't the content of the questions, it was the fact that I had to answer. Keep my answers confined to

까. 예. 그와 파라다이스 여관에 들어간 게 사실입니까. 예. 스스로 먼저 옷을 벗은 게 사실입니까. 예. 재판장님께서도 이런 심문이 경제적이고 기능적이라고 믿으시죠? 예, 라는 짧은 한 음절의 말. 하지만 교도소 앞에 갔었느냐고 물을 때, 내 머릿속엔 온갖, 길고 긴, 어렸을 때의 친정집 뒤란에 있던 우물 두레박줄 같은, 만연체의 문장이 떠올라요. 가령, 우물 곁엔 나이 많은 사철나무 한 그루가 있었는데, 그 그늘이 얼마나 깊은지, 낮에도 침침한 것이 해가 지고 천지사방에 먹물이 스미듯 어둠이 스며들 때면, 그 어둠의 먹물이, 우물 속이나 사철나무 그늘에서 실꾸리의 실이 풀어져 나오는 것처럼 풀어져 나온다고 생각하곤 했어요, 라는 식으로요. 교도소 앞으로 쭈볏쭈볏 다가가 섰을 때, 닫힌 철문에 부딪쳤다가 씽씽 튕겨져 나오는 여름의 아침볕, 그 불화살, 두 눈에 탁탁탁 박혀 올 때, 참을 수 없는 통증으로 질끈 눈을 감고 말았을 때, 바로 그것이 떠올랐거든요.

우물하고 사철나무 말예요.

내가 아마 아홉 살이나 여덟 살, 혹은 일곱 살쯤 됐었던가 봐요. 저기 앉은, 내 간통의, 교도소 앞으로 만나러 간 서, 서, 경, 훈 이장님, 이장님이 소년이었을 때, 경훈

Yes or No, isn't that what you said? I would rather have just remained silent. Yes and No can be such long sentences. Is it true you were in the vicinity of the Gongju Correctional Institute? Yes. Is it true that you entered the Paradise Motel with him? Yes. Is it true that you removed your clothing yourself, of your own accord? Yes. You also believe this kind of questioning to be the most economical and effective, don't you, Your Honor? One short syllable: Yes. But when I am asked if I've been to the vicinity of the prison, what appears in my mind are these long chains of progressive clauses. Such long sentences, each one like the rope from the well in the kitchen garden back at my family's old house when I was a child. Like—the one near that well. There was an old spindle tree, and its shade was so deep and dark, dark even in broad daylight that when the sun went down and the night started to soak, like ink, into the rest of everything, I used to think that this dark ink was coming from inside the well or from the shade of that spindle tree, unwinding itself like thread from a spool. Like that. You see, when I stepped awkwardly up to those closed prison gates, the hot summer sun was hitting the metal and bouncing back, like fiery arrows,

오빠는 내게 말했어요. 사철나무 그늘의 가장자리에 선 채로요. 있잖아, 밤이 어디에서 오냐 하면 말야, 우물에 축축한 검은 옷을 입고 숨어 있다가 말야, 해가 지면 말야, 슬그머니 나와 사철나무 밑에다가 커다란 검은 물레 같은 걸 떠억 갖다 놓고 말야, 이렇게 장대보다 긴 팔로 이렇게, 물레를 돌려서, 연기 피우듯이, 온 세상으로 어둠을 피워 놓걸랑. 그 말을 할 때 그 사람 얼굴의 반은 사철나무 그늘에, 나머지 반은 햇빛 속에 있었어요.

지금도 세심히 기억해요.

밤이 우물 밑에 엎드려 잠자다가 가끔, 눈 비 오거나 뇌성벽력이 치거나 해가 달그림자에 가려 숨죽이고 숨을 때, 한낮에도 바람 쐬러, 아주 가끔, 사철나무 그늘까지 마실도 나온다고, 그는 아주 진정어린 표정으로 내게 설명해 주었습니다. 밤이 축축한 검은 옷을 늘 입고 있는 것은 햇빛과 만나면 죽기 때문이라는 말도 그는 덧붙였지요. 공주교도소 앞에 있었던 게 사실입니까, 라고 저쪽 변호사님이 내게 물어 온 순간, 교도소 앞의 햇빛과, 시멘트 담장과, 철문과, 내 옆의 노파가 들고 있던 두부와, 어떤 젊은 엄마의 등에 업혀 있던 어린것의 자지러지는 울음과, 아카시아나무들, 그리고 그런 것

and when they struck my two eyes, hitting their mark, and I had to squeeze them shut against the unbearable pain, well—that's precisely what came to my mind.

The well and the spindle tree.

I was probably around nine years old, or eight, or maybe closer to seven. The man seated over there, my adulterous lover, the man I went to meet near the prison, Suh, Suh, Gyeong, Hun, village foreman, when the village foreman was a boy, when he was just Gyeong-hun, he told me something. Standing at the edge of the shade of the spindle tree, he said: Hey, so, you know where the night comes from? Well, see, it hides all day in the well, wearing these wet, black clothes, and then, see, when the sun goes down, it creeps out and sets down this big black thing, like a water wheel from a mill or something, right under the spindle tree, and then with its long arm, longer than a lamppost, it starts to spin the wheel around and around, like thiiiiiis, and it spreads the darkness, like smoke, all across the whole world. And as he said all this, his face was half in the shadow of the spindle tree, half in the sunlight.

I remember it exactly, even now.

말고 내 머릿속에 끝없이, 두레박처럼 올라오는 기억들, 예컨대 그가 소년이었을 때 말해준, 검고 축축한 옷을 입은 밤과 사철나무 그늘 따위, 모든 것이 뒤죽박죽, 맞물리고 끈에 꿰인 채 솟아 올라오는데, 그 모든 것을 나는 한 음절로 대답하는 것입니다. 예, 라고요. 그와 파라다이스 여관에 들어간 게 사실입니까, 예, 라고 말예요.

고맙습니다, 재판장님.

마지막 기회라고 하시더니, 나의 긴 만연체를 정말 아무도 막지 않는군요. 말씀드리지요. 예, 아니오라는 짧은 문장으로는 모두 말할 수 없는 내 넋두리. 이렇게 기회를 주시니 뭐라고 감사의 말씀을 드려야 할는지 모르겠습니다. 이래봬도 내 고장에선 여류시인이란 말도 가끔 듣는답니다. 읍에서 문학 동인들이 만드는 동인지의 신인추천작으로 내가 쓴 시가 당선된 게 삼 년 전이에요. 고료는 없었지만 문학소녀였던 내겐 부끄럽고도 큰 기쁨이었어요. 남편은 축하한다며 내게 정장 투피스를 한 벌 사 주었고요. 서 이장님은 체리토마토를 한 바구니나 우리 집 거실 마루에 놓고 갔습니다. 시인이라 불리며 살고 싶었던 내게 이런 덫이 발목을 잡으리라곤 상상도 못했어요. 골프장 공사가 한창 진행되던 때였습

He explained it all to me with the most sincere expression on his face: how the night slept on its stomach at the bottom of the well but how every now and then, when it snowed or rained or there was thunder and lightning or the sun hid quietly behind the shadow of the moon, it might come out for a bit of air in the middle of the day, and how sometimes, just sometimes, it would even come all the way out to the shade of the spindle tree. He added that the reason the night always had to wear such wet, black clothes was that if it ever met the sunlight it would die. Is it true I was in the vicinity of the Gongju Correctional Institute? The instant the other side's lawyer asked me that question, the sunlight in front of the prison gates, the cement wall, the metal door, the tofu in the hand of the old woman standing beside me, the wails of some little child clinging to some young mother's back, the acacia trees, and, aside from all that, all the memories, rising in my mind like endless buckets from a well, like what he had told me as a boy, the black, wet clothes of the night and the shade of the spindle tree, all of it gets mixed up, tangled and fused end to end, gushing up all together, and I am trying to say all of that when I give you my one syllable

니다. 그땐 남편이 이장 일을 맡고 있었지요. 거짓말이라고 할는지 모르겠지만, 어느새 두 아이의 엄마가 된 삼십 대 중반인 그때까지, 나는 밤이 축축한 검은 옷을 입고 한낮엔 깊은 우물 밑에 숨어 지낸다는 걸 믿고 살았습니다. 적어도 감성적으론 그랬지요. 남편이 함부로 두레박을 우물에 던져 넣으면 내가 곧잘 말하곤 했어요. 그러지 마요. 우물 속에 엎드려 있는 그 양반, 두레박에 맞아 잘못하면 허리 다치겠수.

그날이 오기 전까지 나는 어둠이 특별히 무섭거나 혐오스럽다고 여긴 적이 한 번도 없었습니다. 밤이 온다고 완전히 캄캄한 건 아니에요. 순결한, 이런 표현이 가능한지 모르겠지만요, 암튼 이것저것 불순한 빛이 끼여들지 않은 순정의 어둠 속에서 보면, 모든 것들이 제몫, 어떤 빛을 내뿜고 있다고 난 생각해요. 골프장에서 골목 어귀마다 가로등을 설치해주기 전까지, 밤이면 우박처럼 쏴와아, 머리 위로 쏟아져 내리던 별빛이 지금 떠오르네요.

참, 대단한 별빛이었지요.

어디 별빛뿐인가요. 달빛도 우리 동네에서 보면 다르

answer. When I say, Yes. Is it true that I entered the Paradise Motel with him? Yes.

Thank you, Your Honor.

They said this was my last chance, but not one of you is stopping this rambling of mine. So I'll tell you everything. To get this kind of chance to fully air my grievances, which are so impossible to completely contain in these short yes or no statements—I don't know how to thank you. Believe it or not, back home they sometimes call me a lady poet. Three years ago a poem I wrote was chosen for the *Emerging Talent* feature in our town's local literary club magazine. There was no pay, of course, and it was a bit embarrassing, but it meant a lot to me.

I've loved books ever since I was a girl. My husband bought me a nice two-piece dress suit as a congratulations gift, and Foreman Suh left me a basket full of cherry tomatoes at our house. As I dreamed of being called a poet for the rest of my days, I never imagined a trap like this would end up ensnaring me. The golf course construction was in full sway. My husband was the village foreman then. You may not believe this, but even then, even after somehow becoming a thirty-something

다구요. 뒤란의 장독대를 둘러싸고 치자나무 몇 그루 키대기를 하고 있는데요, 그 흰 꽃, 술잔 같은, 여름 깊어 가면서 꽃대도 이파리도 다 덮고 마는 흰 꽃 위로 달빛이, 꼭 만월일 필요는 없고요, 쏟아져 봐요. 뒤란 쪽 문을 가만히 밀어 놓고, 집 안의 불이란 불은 모조리 끄고, 치자꽃 위로 쏟아지는 달빛을 내다보고 있으면 흡, 숨을 막게 된답니다. 어쩌다 마당으로 나설 때면 달빛에 실린 치자꽃 향기가 막무가내 온 실핏줄, 온몸의 모공(毛孔)을 있는 대로 다 열어젖히고 말아요. 내게 화냥기가 있긴 있나 봐요. 왜 치자꽃 향기나 달빛에 매번 모공까지 모두 열리는지 모르겠어요. 별빛도 달빛도 없는 날도 그렇습니다. 치자나무도 그렇고, 옥잠화 너른 잎도 그렇고, 옥잠화 너른 잎이 감싸고 있는 자연석 한 개도 그렇고, 하다못해 추녀 밑에 달아둔 값싼 풍경도 그렇다구요. 빛이 있다구요. 어둠의 온정이라고 할까요, 순결한, 순정의 어둠 속에선 그 빛이 보인다구요. 골프장에서 큰 생색을 내며 가로등을 여기저기 달아주기 전엔 그랬어요. 밤이 돼도 빛이 가득 찬 그런 동네였답니다.

예, 재판장님.

이 재판과 전혀 관계없는 말로 들리신다면 줄이겠습

mother of two, I still believed that the night spent its days wearing wet, black clothes, hiding at the bottom of a deep well. At least, on an emotional level. Sometimes when my husband carelessly tossed the bucket down our well, I'd tell him: "Don't. You might hit the gentleman crouching down at the bottom; if we're not careful the bucket will hurt his back."

Before that day, I never felt any particular fear or disgust towards the dark. The night isn't completely dark, you know. When it's untouched—I don't know if this is the right way to put it, but when the darkness you're in is pure, no taint of this or that little light, well, then you can see the way everything gives off a kind of faint light of its own. That's what I think, anyway. I remember, before the local golf course paid to put up street lights at the mouth of every alley, at night the stars would shine so bright it was as if they might just pour themselves out of the sky and onto your head. Ah, it was really something, that starlight.

And it wasn't just the starlight. The moonlight was different back home, too. Out back, in the kitchen garden, we have a few gardenia trees growing in a

니다. 어둠 속에서도 모든 살아 있는 것이, 사물들이 제 몫몫의 빛을 갖고 있다는 사실이 이 재판과 별 관계가 없다는 재판장님의 지적에 동의할 수는 없지만요.

이야기 전개에 속도를 좀 붙여보도록 할게요.

그날이, 그러니까, 어느 날이냐 하면, 초복을 하루 앞둔, 저기 서경훈 이장님, 애들은 삼촌이라고 부르고 나는 오빠라고 불렀던, 저분이 교도소에서 출감한다고 알려진 그 전날 말인데요, 달은 만월에 가까웠으나 가로등마다 환해서 달빛이고 뭐고 흐리멍텅한데, 몇몇 마을 사람들이 잔뜩 긴장한 표정으로 대청마루에 모여 앉아 있다가 뿔뿔이 흩어져 돌아간 뒤, 홀로 남은 남편이 반 병쯤 남은 마지막 소주병의 소주를 단숨에 들이켜고 나더니, 마당에 불 켜라, 구태여 나에게 하는 말이라곤 느껴지지 않는 한마디 낮은 말, 마당에 불 켜라, 그러고는 마당 가운데 앉아 숫돌에다 낫을 갈기 시작했습니다. 남편은 생각을 깊이 하거나 화가 났을 때, 고통스럽게 참고 견뎌야 할 일이 생겼을 때, 양미간에서 머리까지, 이마를 양분하면서 수직으로 두 줄, 핏줄이 툭 불거져 솟아 올라오곤 하는데요, 그날 밤에도 그랬지요. 가끔 바람이 불면요, 빨랫줄에 매단 갓 씌운 백열등이 흠칫

cluster around all the pickling crocks, and sometimes, in late summer, after all those white blossoms—like little ceramic cups, those blossoms—have fallen, covering the leaves and the stalks and everything, well, the moonlight—it doesn't even have to be full, the moon—just pours down on that blanket of white. Picture it. If you turn off every single light in the house and just push the back door open and stand there, looking out at all that moonlight spilling over all those gardenia blossoms—it just takes your breath away. And if you step out into it, the scent of those gardenias on that moonlight, it'll open you up, open up every capillary under your skin, every pore in your body. I guess they must be right, I must have something of a whore in me. Why else would something like the scent of gardenias or moonlight just open up every pore in me like that, every time? It happens on nights without any moonlight or starlight, too. Just a gardenia tree, or a wide lily leaf, or a stone nestled in that wide lily leaf—even just the sight of a cheap wind chime hanging from the rafters. There's light in them, is what I'm trying to say. You could call it the warmth of the dark, maybe, but in a darkness that's innocent, a darkness that's pure, I'm

흠칫 몸을 떨고, 갈리는 낫날이 백열등 불빛과 만나며, 뭐라고 할까요, 쓰윽, 어둠까지 베고 말, 흰 광채, 쓰윽, 할 때마다 소리 없이 뒤란에서 치자꽃 지고, 엄마 무서워, 큰애 작은애가 내 품 안에 머리를 죽어라고 처박는 것이었습니다.

남편은 오래오래 낫을 갈았지요.

애들을 다독거려 잠재우고 난 후에까지 나는 불 꺼진 거실에 있고, 그이는 백열등 아래 숫돌 앞에 단아하게 앉아 있었어요. 이따금 갈린 낫날을 백열등에 비춰 볼 때 남편의 핏줄은 더욱 불거져 솟아 올라왔습니다. 그이는 무엇을 상상하며 그 낫날을 보았을까요. 단도직입적으로 말해 나는 다음날 교도소에서 출감해 귀가하기로 돼 있는 서경훈 이장님이 무섭진 않았습니다. 물론 그보다 훨씬 전부터 마을 안팎으로 떠돌던 모질고 흉흉한 소문은 나도 듣곤 했지요. 여러 갈래 소문은 하나로 요약됐어요. 요컨대, 서경훈 이장이 출감하여 마을로 돌아오는 날엔 남편이든, 서경훈 이장이든, 둘 중의 한 사람은 살이 찢어지거나 머리가 터져 죽을 수밖에 없다는 것이었습니다. 아니, 한 명이 죽으면 그나마 다행이라고 말하는 사람도 있었지요. 남편과 서경훈 이장을

telling you that you can see it, this light in things. At least, you could, before the golf course so generously put up all those streetlights all over the place. Before that it was the kind of neighborhood that was full of light, even at night.

Yes, Your Honor.

If you really believe all this is unrelated to the trial, I will restrain myself, Your Honor. Even though I can't bring myself to agree that it's not relevant, Your Honor: the fact that everything lives, even in the dark. That every object has its very own light.

Yes, I'll do my best to speed things up.

That day, well, so, that day was actually the day before the first dog days of summer, the day before Foreman Suh Gyeong-hun over there, a man my children call Uncle and I call *Oppa*, or brother—it was the day before we all knew he would be released from prison. The moon was almost full that night, but the streetlights were bright and there was no moonlight to speak of, and a handful of people from around the village had just gone home after they had spent the night sitting, tense-faced, around our open living room. Left by himself, my husband gulped down the last half-full bottle of *soju* and then he called out to me, Turn on the

필두로 해서 마을은 진즉부터 양분돼 있었으니까요. 서경훈 이장의 출감을 앞둔 얼마 전부터 남편을 지지하는 쪽의 몇몇 사람들과, 서경훈 이장 쪽 몇몇 사람들이 읍내로 나가 은밀히 떼로 만나고 있다는 사실 또한 나는 알고 있었습니다. 양쪽 편 사람들은 어쩌다 골목 어귀나 읍내로 나가는 버스에서 부딪칠 때조차 인사를 나누기는커녕 원한에 찬 헛기침을 날리곤 고개를 모로 돌리는 게 보통이었어요.

서 이장 동생이 엽총을 사 왔다는 게야.

어떤 이는 말했습니다.

엽총은 무슨. 도끼날을 갈아 놓으랬대, 서 이장이.

또 어떤 이는 말했습니다. 양쪽 모두 원한이 깊을 대로 깊어, 법이고 뭐고, 서 이장만 출감하면 떼로 죽고 죽일 것이 분명하니, 차라리 서부영화의 흔한 라스트신처럼, 단호하고 간결하게, 둘만의 결투로서 끝장내는 게 그나마 희생을 최소화하는 유일한 방책이 될 거라고 단언하는 사람도 있었습니다. 그가 출감하는 날 전후 며칠이라도 아예 마을을 떠나 피신해 있는 게 좋지 않겠느냐는 충고를 듣기도 했지요. 서 이장을 교도소로 찾아가 만나고 돌아온 사람의 충고였으니 믿을 수밖에요.

front light, he said—that was all he had to say to me, just that low request, Turn on the front light, a thing that hardly counts as saying anything at all, at least to my mind—and with that he just stepped out into to the middle of the yard, sat down, and started sharpening his scythe with a whetstone.

Whenever my husband is deep in thought, or very angry, or when something painful happens that he just has to take and endure, these two veins sprout up, all red and bulging, on either temple—just these pulsing, vertical lines, splitting his forehead into two—and that's what happened that night, too. Every now and then a breeze would blow, and the single, covered light bulb hanging from the clothesline would shudder a bit, swaying from side to side—and when the light from that bulb hit that sharpening scythe blade, it—how to put this—it would glint in the darkness, shhhhhhk, looking like it might slice through the darkness itself, shhhhhhk, and with each pass the gardenias in the back would wilt a little more, and my big one and my little one would both bury their heads deeper into my lap, deeper and deeper, saying Mommy, I'm scared.

My husband sharpened that scythe for a long,

하지만 내가 무서웠던 건 내일이면 돌아올 서 이장님이 아니라, 그 당장, 침묵 속에서, 땀이 밴 이마를 붙박은 듯 정지해 놓고, 마치 뼈를 깎는 고행을 통해 열반에 이르려는 힌두교도처럼, 낫을 갈고 있는 남편이었어요. 남편의 이마를 수직으로 가른 핏줄 두 개는 부풀어 오를 대로 부풀어 올라 터지기 직전으로 보였습니다.

너무 긴장해 있었기 때문일까요.

남편이 낫날을 번쩍 들어 올려 백열등 불빛에 정면으로 비쳐 보려는 순간, 나는 그만 비명을 지르고 말았지요. 여보, 라구요. 내 비명소리는 그랬습니다. 대청마루에서 발작적으로 내려서며 여보, 하고 불렀을 때, 비명처럼요, 낫날로 향하던 남편의 눈빛이 단번에 내게로 날아와 꽂혔습니다.

그 자식, 아직도 좋아하지?

남편의 화살에 찔려 질끈 눈을 감았는데, 그 자식이 말하더라는 거야, 남편은 이어서 날카롭게 갈린 낫날을 내 정수리에 오지게 박아 넣었습니다.

너 때문에 여지껏 장가를 들지 않은 거래.

하얀 치자꽃들이 후두두둑, 한순간, 한꺼번에 목이 잘려 넘어지는 걸 나는 본 듯했어요. 잔인한 낙화였지요.

long time.

Long after I calmed the kids down and put them to bed, I stayed sitting in the darkened living room, and he stayed sitting, stately, under the hanging light bulb, in front of the whetstone. Each time he held the sharpened blade up to the bulb for a closer look, the veins in his temple grew redder, bulging out even more. What was he imagining as he stared at that scythe blade, I wonder? To be completely honest, I wasn't scared at all of Foreman Suh Gyeong-hun, set to come back home after getting released from prison the following day. Of course, by this point, all kinds of crazy rumors had been circulating for a long time already. All the different rumors could basically be broken down into one: in brief, everyone was certain that the day Foreman Suh Gyeong-hun got back to the village, someone, be it my husband or Foreman Suh Gyeong-hun himself, would inevitably end up dead, his head broken open or his flesh torn to pieces.

Actually, there were people who said it would be lucky if only one man ended up dead, considering the number of villagers who had split into two factions, one for my husband and one for Foreman

가로등이, 골프장에서 세워준 가로등이 마을 어귀를 환하게 비추던 한밤에 있었던 일입니다. 모든 게, 마침내, 끝장나는구나. 절망보다 공포감이 내 등덜미를 후려쳤습니다. 여기로 이사 오자고 할 때부터, 뭔가, 꿍꿍이속이 있어서…… 라고 덧붙이다 말고, 남편이 휑하니 대문 밖으로 나갔어요.

사람의 마음이란, 정말, 모를 일이에요.

정말 모르겠어요, 재판장님. 친정집이 있던 고향마을이라고 하지만요, 이미 양친께서 작고하셨고 동생들마저 집 팔고 논 팔아 대처로 떠났으니, 마을에, 특별히 의지하고 살 사람이 따로 있었던 건 아닙니다. 오촌고모가 한 분 계시지만 치매로 날 알아보지도 못하시구요, 어릴 적 친구들도 오래전 모두 떠나갔구요, 마을 어귀의 느티나무들도 일부는 베어져 그루터기만 남았습니다.

벌써 육 년 전의 일이네요.

남편은 본래 중견 건설회사에서 경리 담당으로 일하는 사람이었어요. 아주 꼼꼼하고 성실하고 과묵한 타입이었지요. 우리가 처음 만날 때, 나는 여상을 졸업하고 은행창구에서 일한 지 삼 년을 막 넘기고 있었습니다. 남편은 중요한 고객 중 한 분이었어요. 어느 날 지점장

Suh. I knew myself that starting some time before Foreman Suh was set to be released, a few people in my husband's camp and a few people in Suh Gyeong-hun's camp had taken to holding secret meetings outside the village, in town. And when people from one side ran into people from the other, on the street somewhere or on a bus into town, not only did they not say hello to each other, but also they would clear their throats and actually turn their backs on one another. This had become commonplace.

I hear Foreman Suh's little brother bought a hunting rifle.

That's what one person said.

Don't be ridiculous, there's no hunting rifle. I hear Foreman Suh told him to sharpen the axe.

That's what someone else said. There was even someone who said that since resentment had grown as much as it was going to grow on both sides, and since, law or no law, it looked as though a whole bunch of people were going to be killed once Foreman Suh got out of prison, the only way to minimize the loss of life would be to go the way of the final scene in some old American Western and just have the two men duel it out, short and

이 나를 지목해 남편의 회사로 심부름을 보낸 게 구체적 인연의 시작이 되었습니다. 서류가방을 들고 합정동 로터리 근처의 남편 회사를 찾아가면서, 왜 하필 창구에서 일하는 내게 심부름을 시키나 하고 잠시 생각했어요. 그것도 퇴근시간이 다 돼서요. 창구 일을 하면 퇴근시간에 온갖 것을 확인하고 대조해보랴, 더 바쁘거든요. 뒷일 걱정 말고 거기 들렀다가 그냥 퇴근해도 좋아, 라고 지점장님은 말했습니다. 과묵한데다가 곧잘 내 앞에서 얼굴을 붉히기도 했던 남편이, 사랑의 속병을 앓다 못해 지점장에게 부탁해 일부러 꾸민 일이라곤 전혀 상상도 못했지요. 그도 그럴 것이, 나는 꽃다운 스물두 살이었거든요.

합정동 근처의 어느 일식집이 떠오르네요.

내가 젓가락질을 하기 기다렸다가 한점 한점, 생선회를 나의 앞접시에 놓아주던 그날의 남편 말이에요. 정작 자신은 별로 먹지도 않으면서, 요것은 광어, 요것은 우럭, 일일이 설명해주면서 내가 입에 넣기도 전에 벌써 다른 생선회를 들고 기다리던 남편의 모습은 참 순수하고 다정해 뵀습니다. 남편은 그때 스물아홉 살이었지요. 나이 차이가 많은 게 좀 걸리기도 했지만, 그날부

sure. Another asked me if it wouldn't be best to, at least, leave the village for a little while, just for a few days before and after his release. And that was from someone who'd been to the prison to meet with Foreman Suh, so I had to think they knew what they were talking about. But you know, what actually scared me wasn't Foreman Suh's return the following day; it was the man in front of me in that very moment, sitting in silence, his still forehead covered in sweat, grinding and grinding that scythe against that whetstone like some devout Hindu seeking nirvana through some excruciating path of penance: my husband. The throbbing veins dividing his forehead were bulging so hard they seemed about to burst.

Maybe it was because I was so nervous?

As my husband raised the scythe blade to the light of the bulb to get a better look, I heard myself shriek. Darling, I said. That's what I screamed out. And as I hurried down from the open living room into the yard, calling out, Darling, like I was screaming out to him, my husband's gaze flew from the blade of the scythe and out to me, and struck, like an arrow shot from a bow.

That bastard—you still love him, don't you?

터 일 년 후 우린 결혼했습니다. 이태가 지나서 첫애를 얻었고, 첫애 얻고 삼 년 만에 둘째 애를 얻었어요. 아파트를 장만하려고 청약예금도 부지런히 부었고요, 콩나물 값까지 아껴 정기적금도 꼬박꼬박 넣었습니다. 남편이 혈혈단신이나 다름없어 좀 외롭고 좀 가난했지만요, 남들이 다 사는 순차대로, 또박또박, 도란도란, 알콩달콩, 우린 살았는데요, 어떤 날, 불현듯 남편의 회사가 부도를 내면서부터 모든 게 뒤죽박죽되기 시작했습니다. 경리 책임자였던 남편도 책임져야 할 일이 있었지요. 몇 달 간 지방으로 어디로 숨어 지내다가 자수하여, 비록 두 달도 채 안 된 기간이었지만, 옥살이도 했습니다. 회귀본능이라고들 말하는데, 실패하지 않으면 사람들은 뒤돌아설 줄 몰라요. 앞으로 앞으로 죽을 둥 살 둥 꿈같이 나아가는 거지요. 남편의 회사가 망한 것만 해도 그렇습니다. 그냥 건설회사만 성실히 꾸려갔더라면 아무 문제도 없을 거라고들 말하데요. 아파트 좀 짓고 해서 큰돈 만지게 되니까 옳거니, 나도 잘하면 정주영이 될 수 있겠구나, 그만 이것저것, 왕창왕창, 사업을 벌이다가 망한 경우지요.

다들 그렇지 않나요?

Struck by this arrow from my husband, I squeezed my eyes shut. But he went on. They say that's what he's telling people, and then he took that scythe's sharpened blade and drove it, hard, into the heart of the crown of my head.

They say you're the reason he still isn't married.

It felt as though I was watching all those white gardenias fall as one to the ground in a heap, each slender neck sliced through in one fell swoop. A cruel scattering of blossoms. It was late by then, an hour when the streetlights—put up by the golf course—were shining bright at the village entrance. Ah, I realized. It's all, finally, going to be over. What came over me then was closer to fear than desperation. I should have known something was going on from the moment you started saying you wanted to move here... and just like that, trailing off there, my husband stepped out the front gate.

The human heart, it's so—it's unknowable.

I honestly couldn't say, Your Honor. I suppose it is my hometown, since that's where my family was from, but my parents have already passed away and my siblings have all sold their homes and farms to move to bigger cities—so it's not as if there was anyone in particular left in the village whom I could

아이엠에프가 오기 전까지 우리가 배운 거라곤 그저 가야 한다, 뜀박질로 가야 한다, 이것저것, 이놈저놈, 밀어내고, 밟고, 죽이고라도 가야 한다, 그뿐이었는걸요. 큰아이가 학교 갈 때쯤 애들이 잘 부르던 노래가 있어요. 앞으로, 앞으로, 앞으로 앞으로, 하던 씩씩하고 우렁찬 노래요. 그 노래만 들으면 진저리가 쳐지는데 남편은 틈만 나면, 더욱 우렁차게 해야지, 격려 고무 질책하면서, 그 노래만 애한테 시키는 거예요. 그러고 보면 고향 동네로 이사 간 것이 내게는 일종의 회귀였는데, 남편은 잠시 엎드려 찬스를 보자는, 일종의 전략이었는지도 모르겠어요.

그게 아마 칠월 하순쯤 됐었나 봐요.

밤낮없이 무더위가 기승을 부렸으니깐요. 옥살이하는 남편을 면회하고 돌아오는데 불현듯, 정말 뜬금없이, 타는 듯한 갈증이 나면서요, 뭔가, 쑤욱, 땅 밑 지구 중심으로부터요, 쑤우욱, 눈앞으로 솟아 올라오는데요, 그게 글쎄, 우물이었어요. 친정집 뒤란에 있던 우물 말예요. 축축한 검은 옷을 입고 밤이 엎드려 숨어 산다고 해서 행여 부정적으로 상상하진 마세요.

향기가 난다면 믿으시겠어요들?

count on, or whom I could go to. I have a great-aunt, but she suffers from dementia—she doesn't even recognize me anymore—and all my old childhood friends left town long ago. Even the grove of zelkova trees at the town entrance isn't the same anymore—so many have been cut down, just their stumps left behind.

It was already six years ago now.

My husband was the head of accounting at a mid-grade construction company. He was very exact, and dutiful, and taciturn—you know the type of man I mean. When we first met, I had just passed the three-year mark at the bank, working as a teller—my first job after graduating from the vocational girls' high school. He was one of our most important clients. Then one day the head of our branch sent me over to his office with some papers, and that was the start of our actual connection. As I looked for his office building, over near the Hapjeong-dong Rotary, I wondered, briefcase in hand, why on earth they'd sent me, a teller who should have been at her window—and so close to the end of the work day, too. When you're working at the bank window, closing time is actually the busiest part of the day, you see—all kinds of things

정말이에요. 특히 신새벽 우물가로 가 보면요, 모락모락 김이 나는데요, 그 김에 아주 부드러운 향기가 깃들여 있어요. 친정집 우물만 그런 게 아니에요. 우리 동네는 예로부터 워낙 물이 좋은 걸로 호가 나서 동네 이름도 아예 정수리지요. 누구네 집이랄 것 없이 우물이 있는 집에선 다 향기가 났습니다. 물 향기가요. 나는 비틀거리면서, 잰걸음으로, 남편이 갇힌 감옥을 등지고 걸었습니다. 버스정류장까지 끈질기게 친정집 우물이 날 따라오데요. 음료수를 사서 마셨으나 아무 소용없었어요. 갈증은 점점 심해져서 나중엔 입 안이 온통 갈라지는 것 같았지요.

또 모를 일입니다.

그 우물에의 기억과 함께, 그 순간, 서 이장님, 오빠라고 불렀던 저분이 생각났었는지도. 남편은 내가 첨부터 계획적으로 우리 동네에 이사 갈 집을 구했다고 하는데요. 세상에, 마치 그때부터 이미 서 이장님하고 내가 눈 맞추고 배 맞추었다고 주장하고 싶은 눈치지만요, 세상에, 그것이 말도 되지 않는다는 건 남편이 더 잘 알고 있을 거라고 봐요. 내가 확신할 수 없는 것은 그날 고향으로 찾아가며 서 이장님 생각을 했었던가, 하는 거예요.

to double-check and confirm.

Don't worry about wrapping up and just consider this errand the end of your day, is what the branch head had told me. I never even imagined that it was all a plan, that my husband, so quiet, and rather prone to blushing when we spoke, had been pining and pining after me until he could pine no more, and that he had finally asked the branch manager for a favor. Though, you know, it's not difficult to see why; I was a flower of a girl back then, just barely twenty years old.

I'm remembering, now, this one Japanese restaurant near Hapjeong-dong.

I'm remembering my husband that day, the way he would wait for me to eat a piece of sashimi and put another on my plate, one after another. The way he explained, This one is halibut, This one is soft-shell clam, naming each new piece and picking the next one up with his chopsticks before the last was even in my mouth, all without even eating much himself; it all seemed so naïve, felt so gentle. He was twenty-nine years old. I did worry a bit about the age difference, but we were married just a year later. Two years later we had our first child, and three years after that we had our second. We

친정집을 싸리문 밖에서 돌아보곤 곧 서 이장님, 그러니까 경훈 오빠 집으로 갔으니까요.

글쎄요. 이런 생각도 해 봅니다.

불현듯 고향집을 찾아가 본 것이야, 인지상정, 삶이 고단하고 세상 얼음처럼 차가우니 어쩌다 그럴 수 있다고 치고, 그러나 만약 그곳에서 경훈 오빠를 안 만났더라면, 순박하고 따뜻한 눈빛과 진정어린 말씨로 나를 맞아주었던 저분이 없었더라면, 그곳으로 돌아가 터 잡고 살 생각을 했을까 하구요. 고향집 우물은 그대로 있었으나 집은 새로 지어 딴집 같았고 사람들도 모두 낯설었어요. 서울에서 한 시간 반이면 가 닿는 풍광 좋은 곳이라서 그런지, 그동안 이사 들어온 낯선 사람이 생각보다 많았거든요. 솔직히 말씀드리자면, 고향집을 둘러볼 때보다도 친정 오라버니 같은 서 이장님을 만났을 때, 비로소 고향에 돌아왔다는 걸 실감할 수 있었어요.

돌아보면 그래요.

내 어린 시절의 따뜻한 삽화들 중 반쯤엔 경훈 오빠가 들어 있어요. 옆집에 사는데다가 우리 집 우물을 같이 썼으므로, 학교 갈 때도 그렇고, 집에서도 그렇고, 노상 함께 노는 시간이 많았으니깐요. 성격이 다감한데다

worked hard, putting money aside toward an apartment application fee, spending as little as possible, even on our bean sprouts so we could pay into our installment savings. My husband was practically an orphan so we were a bit poor and things were a bit lonely, but we lived as well as anyone does, a chatty, happy family, building our lives one step at a time. Until one day, out of nowhere, my husband's company went bankrupt—and that's when everything started to go sideways.

It turned out that as the head of accounting, my husband had his share of responsibility in what happened, and so we all had to go into hiding for a few months, down in the country, until he turned himself in. He even went to prison himself, though it was only for two months. They say it's instinctive, the call to go home, but you know, people who haven't failed don't know how to turn back. They just keep going forward, forward, not quite living, not quite dead, just moving forward as if they're in some kind of trance. You could say the same about my husband's company folding the way it did. They say if the company had just stuck to its original construction business, none of this would have happened. Build a few apartments and see some

가, 오빠는 특히 손재주가 많아서, 개울가로 산으로 날 데리고 다니며 온갖 것을 만들어 주곤 했어요. 호드기도 만들어 주었고요, 인형을 나무로 깎아준 적도 있었고요, 눈썰매도 짜 주었지요. 내 공작숙제는 매번 오빠 차지였습니다. 고등학교를 들어가기 위해 오빠가 먼저 동네를 떠났고, 내가 여상에 합격한 이태 뒤엔 나도 떠났습니다. 사실은 떠나기 전부터, 그러니까 오빠의 턱에 거뭇거뭇 수염이 돋아나고부터, 뭔지 어색해졌다고 할까요, 우리 관계가 전과 같지 않았지만요. 오빠가 떠나기 전날 밤이던가, 두 뼘은 됨직한 참나무로 깎은 장승 한 쌍을 내게 준 일이 지금 생각나네요. 너 잠잘 때 무섭다고 해서 말야, 방문 앞에 이걸 두고 자면 안 무서울 거야. 서울로 떠나면서 장승은 갖고 가지 않았어요. 괜히 유치한 장난 같았거든요. 참, 여고 다닐 때 한번, 오빠가 학교로 찾아온 일이 있어요. 눈이 퀭하고 예전보다 훨씬 깡마른 모습이었는데요, 집안 형편 때문에 학교를 그만두고 공군에 자원입대할 예정이다, 뭐 그런 말 했던 게 기억나요. 나는 좀 짜증을 부렸었지요. 학교로 찾아오니까 친구들 보기에도 창피하고 해서요. 다시는 안 올 테니까 걱정 마라, 라고 그가 말했던 것 같아

real money and you think, That's right, If I just play my cards right I can become another Jung Joo-yung, I can become the next Kim Woo-joong. And so you keep rolling the dice until one day, in the blink of an eye, it all comes tumbling down.

Isn't everyone like that, really?

If you think about it, before the IMF came to Korea, that was all we were taught that we had to keep going, had to run, had to sprint, stepping on whatever, whoever stood in our way, killing them if we had to. There was a song the children liked to sing, back when my oldest first started school. A tough, energetic little song that went, Forward, forward, forward forward forward! I couldn't stand it, after a while, but my husband would egg him on to sing it over and over at every turn, encouraging him, berating him: Sing it louder! More energy! Come to think of it, even though moving back to my old village was a homecoming, of sorts, for me, for my husband it might have been more strategic: a place to lay low for a spell while he looked for his next opportunity.

It was towards the end of July, I think.

Because the heat was sweltering, night and day. I was on my way back from visiting my husband in

요, 지금 생각해 보니까.

왜 그렇게 눈물이 나왔던지요.

옛집은 흔적 없이 사라지고 낯선 벽돌집이 버티고 선 우리 집 대문간을 서성이다가 행여 그가 있을까, 서 이장님 싸리문 앞으로 다가갔을 때요, 누가 문을 쓱 열고 나오는데, 바로 경훈 오빠였어요. 거기…… 미현이 아녀, 라고 저쪽에서 먼저 말했지요. 그 순간, 갑자기, 눈물샘이 터진 것처럼, 막 눈물이 나는 거예요. 어린 시절, 너무 억울하고 분한 꼴을 당하고 집으로 돌아오다가, 어머니나 아버지를 만나면 말보다 앞서 눈물이 앞을 가리듯이요. 오빠가 자신의 집 마루로 데려다가 앉혀 놓고 서늘한 물수건을 손에 들려줄 때까지도 눈물이 그치질 않았어요. 나는 물을 마셨지요. 너 예전에 살던 집, 그 뒤란의 우물물이야, 라고 그가 말했고요. 그 말을 듣자마자 눈물 뚝 그치면서, 내가 대꾸를 했습니다.

오빠 나 예 와서 살까 봐.

내 자신에게도 참으로 뜻밖의 말이었어요.

정말야, 오빠. 빈집 같은 거, 없을까.

한 번 떠난 말은, 말(馬)처럼, 앞으로 내달리기 마련인가 봐요. 말만 앞으로 내달리는 게 아니라 마음도 내달

prison when suddenly, I mean really suddenly, from nowhere, my throat started burning, parched, and something just—whoosh, from the center of the earth, whoosh, surged up in front of me. It was a well. I'm telling you, it was the well that used to be in the back kitchen garden at my family's old house. Don't imagine it to be a bad thing, either, just because I said the night crouches down inside it wearing damp, black clothes.

Would you all believe me if I said I could smell it? It's true. Especially when you went out to it right at dawn, at very first light, there would be a kind of vapor coming off of it, and that vapor—it had this incredibly soft fragrance to it. It wasn't just the well at my family's old house that has this scent, either. Our neighborhood has always been famous for having good water, so much so that it's actually called "Jeongsu-ri," Clear Water Village. And every house with a well, no matter whose house it was, had that same scent. The scent of water.

Staggering from side to side, practically limping, I kept going, the prison holding my husband behind me. Our old family well followed me all the way to the bus stop. I stopped and bought myself a soda to drink, but it was no use. I just got thirstier and

려가는 걸 느꼈습니다. 한번 오빠라고 부르고 나니까, 신기할 정도로 단번에 곡절 많은 시간들 싹 지워 없어지고, 오빠와 나 사이, 스스럼없이 어린 시절로 돌아가버리는 것이었어요. 오빠, 나무인형 하나 깎아줘, 라고까지 말할 수 있을 것 같았습니다.

그렇게 된 것입니다, 재판장님.

옥살이를 마치고 나온 남편은, 내가 고향 동네에 빈집 하나를 구해놨다고 하자 군말 없이 이삿짐을 쌌습니다. 치자꽃이 다 지기도 전이었어요. 남편은 지쳐 있었고 나는 새 꿈을 꾸었습니다. 집을 고치는 일부터 비닐하우스를 할 농토를 싼값에 빌려 얻는 것까지, 서 이장님이 다 앞장섰습니다. 남편과 경훈 오빠는 정말 죽이 잘 맞았다고 나는 지금도 생각해요. 친처남매부보다 더 가까웠지요. 남편이 불과 이 년 만에 동네 이장을 맡을 정도로 빨리 적응할 수 있었던 것도 그렇습니다. 원래 인심 좋은 동네이기도 했지만요. 남편과 경훈 오빠의 두터운 우정이 없었다면 그렇게 빨리 터를 잡지는 못했을 거라고 봐요. 가난했지만 우린 행복했습니다. 비닐하우스에 선인장을 재배해서, 이 년 만에, 밭도 팔백 평이나 장만할 수 있었고, 치자나무 밑에 우물도 팠습니다. 어

thirstier until finally it felt as though the whole inside of my mouth was cracking apart.

Who knows what that meant.

It's possible that in that moment, along with the memory of that well, I might have also thought of Foreman Suh, the gentleman over there that I once called *Oppa*. My husband insists that I planned it all along, that the whole move back home was part of this plan. Can you imagine? He clearly wants to suggest that this was when Foreman Suh and I first got together, that this was when we started sleeping together, can you even imagine that? I can tell you, my husband knows better than anyone else that none of that is true. What I can't tell you for sure is whether or not I thought of Foreman Suh as I headed back to my old village that day.

You see, after I went by the old family house and looked in the front gate, I went straight to Foreman Suh's house—that is, I went straight to Gyeonghun *Oppa*'s house. I don't know. A thought does occur to me, though. I mean, suddenly deciding to go back to my old family home like that, that could have been an understandable reaction to the exhaustion of daily life, to the ice coldness of the world at large. But it strikes me now that if I hadn't

렸을 땐 그리도 깊어 뵈는 우물이었는데요. 열 자도 파지 않아 향기로운 물이 콸콸 쏟아져 나왔어요.

작두샘은 싫어, 여보.

내 고집을 남편은 기꺼이 들어주었지요.

황등쑥돌을 괴어 우물을 만들고 예전처럼 두레박을 매달 철제 구조물도 만들었습니다. 두레박은 경훈 오빠가 만들어 주었지요. 우물이 완성된 날 풍물패, 마당 가득, 날라리젓대 앞세워 돌아가고, 뒤뜰에선 똑, 똑 치자꽃 지고, 노세노세 젊어서 노세, 마을 사람들이 막걸리에 취해 어깨동무하고 노래하던 모습이 눈에 선합니다. 정수리는 물만 맑은 동네가 아닙니다. 우물에서만 향기가 나는 곳이 또 아닙니다. 향기 나는 우물을 마음에 하나씩 품고 사는 사람들이 사는 동네예요. 개발이다 뭐다 험한 세월 살았다지만 우리 정수리는 달랐습니다. 뒤떨어지지 않았으면서도 고요했지요. 남쪽 산 너머에 수백 대씩 트럭들이 드나들고 밤낮없이 중장비가 산을 깎아 골프장 공사가 시작되기 전까지 그랬다구요. 해마다 한 번씩 동제가 열리는 동네도 근동에선 우리 정수리밖에 없었습니다. 젊은 사람들이 다투어 도시로 나가고 나이든 어른들이나 고향을 지키고 사는 세태야 다른

seen Gyeong-hun *Oppa* that day, if he hadn't been there, with his simple, warm gaze and his sincere turns of speech, who knows if I would still have thought to move back for good. The well out back was still there, but the house had been rebuilt and felt completely different, and all the people felt like strangers. Maybe because it's a scenic area close to Seoul, just an hour and a half away, but it was clear that all kinds of strangers had moved to the village in the time I'd been gone. To be completely honest, more than when I looked around the house I grew up in, it was when I saw Foreman Suh, this man who had been like a real brother to me, that I truly felt I had come back home.

I see that now, looking back.

Gyeong-hun *Oppa* is in one out of every two warm memories I have of my childhood. Not only did he live next door, his family shared our well with us, and so whether we were at school or at home, we were almost always playing together. He was a sensitive boy, and good with his hands, and he would take me along to the creek or up in the hills and make me all kinds of things to play with. He made me a reed pipe once, and carved me a doll out of wood, and built me a sled for the snow.

동네와 다를 것 없었으나, 다른 동네와 달리, 우리 정수리는 일손이 턱없이 모자라지도 않았습니다. 농번기 때는 주말마다, 도시로 나가 사는 젊은 자식들, 일손 돕겠다고 열 일 다 제치고 돌아오기 때문이었지요. 효자가 많은 동네였는데요. 사람들은 너나없이 물이 좋아서 그렇다고 했습니다. 주민들이 모두 유순하고 후덕한 것도 물이 좋아서라는 것입니다. 물론 국도에서 산굽잇길로 십 리나, 외통수 길을 들어가서 자리 잡고 있다는 지리적 환경 때문에 개발의 모진 바람을 덜 탔다고 할 수도 있지만, 나는 지금도 믿고 있어요. 물이 좋아서 효자가 많이 나고, 물이 좋아서 인심이 후했다는 어르신네들 말씀을요. 사람 몸의 대부분이 물로 되어 있다잖아요. 맑고 향기 나는 물이 언제나 몸속에 꽉 차 있어 봐요. 영혼도 절로 정화되지 않을까요.

그날 얘기로 돌아가야 되겠군요.

예, 교도소 앞으로 찾아갔던 날의 자초지종을 말씀드려야겠지요. 서 이장님은 출감한다는 날 돌아오지 않았습니다. 서 이장님을 마중 갔던 동생이 혼자 돌아와 사무 착오로 날짜가 잘못 전해졌다고 하더랍니다. 서 이

Any origami homework I had was always *Oppa*'s job to complete. *Oppa* left home first, to go to high school, and two years after that I left, too, after getting into the vocational girls' school. Although, you know, even before that things had started to feel different, a little awkward, somehow—ever since the first faint strands of *Oppa*'s beard started coming in. I remember now—maybe the night before he left, or at least sometime around then—*Oppa* gave me a pair of Jangseung totems he had carved out of oak. Because you said you get scared when you have to go to bed, he'd told me. If you hang these on your door you won't be scared anymore. When I left for Seoul I didn't take the totems with me. It seemed childish, then.

Ah, actually, there was this one time that *Oppa* came to see me at my school. His eyes were sunken and he was much thinner than before. I remember he told me he'd had to quit school because his family had fallen on hard times, that he was going to volunteer and join the air force or something like that. I was a little cross with him. It was embarrassing, having him come to my school like that. I think he told me not to worry, that he wouldn't ever come see me again. I think that's what he said,

장님이 출감한 날은 통고받은 날보다 하루 뒤였던 것이지요. 종일 뭔가, 가파르게 다가올 운명적 파멸을 기다리듯 말없이 집을 지키고 있던 남편은, 다 저물녘, 어디에선가 걸려온 전화를 받더니 외출복을 찾아 입는 것이었습니다.

어디 좀 다녀와야겠어.

남편은 혼잣말하듯 말했습니다.

내일 밤에야 올 것 같다고, 기다리지 말고 자라는 말을 덧붙일 때에도 남편은 내게 시선을 주지 않았어요. 푹 꺼진 눈자위가 어둡고 섬찟해 보이더라구요. 눈은 핏발이 잔뜩 서 있구요. 눈동자는 불안하게 뭔가를 찾는 듯했습니다. 전날 밤부터 우린 한마디도 대화를 나누지 않은 상태였어요. 어디를 가시느냐 물어야 할 일인데, 말은 입 밖으로 나가지 않고요, 귓속에 둥둥둥, 전날 밤 남편이 마지막으로 내뱉은 말, 여기로 이사 오자고 할 때부터 뭔가…… 라던 말이 이명으로 울고 있었습니다. 남편은 신발끈을 오래오래 조여 묶었고, 나는 벙어리처럼 그걸 보고 있을 뿐이었지요. 밤이 왔는데도 기온은 전혀 떨어지지 않아, 찌는 듯 더웠습니다.

대문 앞까지 갔던 남편이 뒤돌아서 헛간 앞으로 걸어

thinking back now.

I wonder why I cried so.

When I saw that our old house had been torn down and replaced with some strange new brick thing I walked over and approached the front gate of Foreman Suh's own house—after hanging around the front gate for a little while—and then, wondering if maybe he was still around, well, who might be stepping out at that exact moment if not Gyeong-hun *Oppa* himself? He was the one who spoke first: It's...it's Mi-hyeon, isn't it? And suddenly, as if my tear ducts had all burst at once, I was weeping. It was just like when I was a child, walking home after an awful, frustrating day. If I ran into my mother or father I would just burst into tears before I could even get a word out about it. It was just like that. I couldn't stop, either. I just kept on crying as *Oppa* brought me in and sat me down in his open living room and placed a cool, wetted handkerchief in my hand. I drank some water. It's well water, he told me. From the well behind your old house. The second I heard those words my tears stopped, just like that, and I replied.

Oppa, I'm thinking of moving back here.

It startled me, too, this declaration.

가데요.

그때 나는 보았지요. 헛간 안에서 남편이 들고 나온 것은 전날 밤 마당 가운데 앉아 숫돌에 갈았던 낫날이었습니다. 낫이 아니라 낫날요. 언제 그렇게 해 두었는지, 낫은 손잡이에서 빠져나와 맨몸뚱어리더라구요. 손잡이에 찔려져 있던 곳은 테이프로 친친 감겨 손으로 잡을 수 있게 만들어져 있었습니다. 남편은 그것을 수건으로 둘둘 감아 뒷주머니에 쑤셔 넣고 나갔습니다. 내게 보란 듯이요.

물론 잠을 잘 수 없었지요.

길고, 무덥고, 무서운 하룻밤이었지요.

새벽 첫차를 타고서 읍내로 나왔고요, 공주교도소 정문 앞에 도착한 것은 아홉 시 사십 분쯤 됐습니다. 수위 아저씨가 출옥자는 열 시가 조금 넘으면 나올 거라고 하데요. 나는 당연히 서 이장님의 동생이 마중을 오리라고 생각했었지요. 그러나 열 시가 돼도 교도소 앞엔 낯익은 얼굴이 전혀 없었습니다. 열 시에서 십 분쯤이나 넘겼을까요. 철문이 열렸구요. 두부에 쪽박까지 든 사람들이 우르르 철문 앞으로 몰려갔구요, 그리고 그가 나왔습니다. 골프장 마크가 선명하게 찍힌 셔츠를 입고

I'm serious, *Oppa*. Do you know if there are any empty houses around here?

Once you say a thing, it really does take on a life of its own. And it's not just the words that have been said but the heart that says it, too. Now that I'd called him *Oppa*, it was astonishing, the way all those years of ups and downs disappeared. The way *Oppa* and I, we seemed to just settle comfortably back into how it had been for us as children. I felt like I could just turn to him and say: *Oppa*, carve me a doll, would you?

That's how it happened, Your Honor.

My husband was released after finishing his prison term, and when I told him I'd found us a house in my old hometown, he just started packing up our things without a word of protest. From fixing up the new house to getting cheap rent on a plot of land to building our vinyl greenhouse, Foreman Suh took the lead on everything. Even now, there's no doubt in my mind that my husband and Gyeong-hun *Oppa* really clicked as friends. They were closer than most family. It's how my husband adjusted to country life so completely. So much so that in just two years he became a Village Foreman himself.

말이에요.

세상에, 거기서 또 골프장을 보다니요.

그가 입고 있는 것은 재작년이던가, 골프장 직원용으로 만들었다가 특별히 마을 사람들에게까지 나누어 준 그 셔츠였습니다. 그 셔츠가 나올 때만 해도 남편이 이장이었지요. 재판장님도 이미 들어서 알고 계시지만, 우리 동네는 2년마다 한 번씩, 민주적 방식으로 이장 선거를 하고, 연임은 얼마든지 할 수 있어요. 서 이장님이 딱 한 표가 많아 남편을 이기고 이장이 되기 전까지, 남편은 2년 임기의 이장을 두 번 연임했습니다. 경리 업무를 한데다가 워낙 꼼꼼하고 공평했으므로, 타고난 이장이라고들 했습지요. 골프장이 들어서지 않았으면 남편은 아마 지금도 이장 일을 보고 있을 것입니다.

다 아시는 얘기라도 들어주세요, 재판장님.

골프장이 들어선다 했을 때 흔히 그렇듯이, 마을 사람 의견은 제각각이었습니다. 마을기금으로, 골프사업자는 공사가 시작되기도 전에 삼천만 원을 내놨는데요, 시골 사람들에겐 적은 돈이 아니었지요. 가가호호 나누자는 의견도 있었고 마을 공공기금으로 놔두자는 말도 있었습니다. 애당초 골프장 건설을 반대해야 한다고 주

It's a welcoming sort of community to start with, certainly, but without the closeness that sprang up between him and Gyeong-hun *Oppa*, there's just no way my husband could have made a place for himself so quickly. We were poor, but we were happy. We cultivated cacti in our vinyl greenhouse, and in just two years we were able to procure an eight hundred *pyeong* stretch of land for ourselves. That's where we dug our well, right by a gardenia tree. Wells all seemed so deep back when I was young, but we only had to dig ten feet or so before that fragrant water came gushing forth.

I don't want a pump, Darling; I want a real well.

My husband indulged this stubbornness of mine.

We built the well out of mugwort rocks and constructed the steel structure for hanging the bucket. The bucket itself Gyeong-hun *Oppa* made for us. I still remember the day we finished the well: we hired a *pungmul* troupe, and as they danced and played in the yard, piper in the lead, the gardenias withering quietly out back, chanting Dance, Dance, Dance while we're young, all the villagers, drunk on rice wine, sang and swayed with their arms around each other's shoulders. I can still see it all.

Jeongsu-ri is a neighborhood with more than just

장하는 사람도 있었지만요, 삼천이라는 거금이 들어오자 반대의견은 흐지부지되고, 그 대신 돈을 어떻게 쓸지로 의견이 양분되데요. 골프장 측에선 공사가 끝나고 돈을 더 내놓겠다고 했어요. 마을은 그야말로 호떡집에 불난 것처럼 떠들썩해졌습니다. 캐디로 나서겠다는 젊은 아낙도 있었습니다. 공사가 시작되고 나선 논밭에서 일하던 사람들이 너나없이 골프장 공사현장으로 나갔습니다. 농사짓는 것보다 그쪽 임금이 훨씬 나았으니깐요.

모든 것이 마치 바람 좋은 봄날의 산불처럼 삽시간에 번졌어요.

공사가 본격적으로 시작되고 나자 수없이 드나드는 트럭들과 현장의 산을 깎아내는 흙먼지 때문에 빨래조차 널 수 없을 지경이 됐습니다. 그래도 마을 사람들은 별 불평이 없었어요. 가가호호 하루 몇 만 원씩 빳빳한 현찰이 들어왔거든요. 도시에 사는 어떤 분들에겐 푼돈이겠지만요, 대대로 고추농사나 담배농사 주로 하며 살아온 외진 정수리에서, 한 가구 두 사람이 일 나가면 매일 십만 원씩 현찰이 들어오는데, 반대고 자시고, 눈 돌아가지 않을 사람이 어디 있겠습니까. 더구나 우리 동네만은 특별 배려를 해서 예순을 넘긴 지 한참 된 노인

clear water. It's a place where each person lives with a fragrant well sheltered in his or her heart. It's a hard time we're living in now, with all this redevelopment and whatnot. But Jeongsu-ri was different. It was quiet without being backwards. At least, it was until they started construction on the golf course, carving into the mountain with all their heavy equipment and sending those huge trucks, hundreds of them, up and down the southern slopes, day and night.

We even had a winter festival every year—Jeongsu-ri was the only place for miles that still did that. The young people still left for the big city and the elders were still left behind, just like any other country village, but still, unlike those other places, our Jeongsu-ri didn't have any huge shortage of workers. Because, you see, every weekend in the busy seasons, all the young sons and daughters out living in the cities would come back to help. It was a village with devoted children, and everyone agreed this was because of the water. They say the water is why all the villagers are gentle and generous, too. Of course, you could argue that, being miles down a windy mountain road from the nearest highway, we were just naturally spared the

까지도 일당 오만 원씩으로 일감을 주었습니다. 그런 노인들이 무슨 일을 하겠어요. 그저 일하는 흉내를 내다가 일당 받아오면 그뿐이고, 골프장 쪽에선 유일한 동네, 정수리 사람들 다독거리면 그뿐이고, 누이 좋고 매부 좋고 하는 거지요. 남편은 노인들까지도 일당을 받고 일하게 된 건 전적으로 이장인 자신의 공이라고 큰소리를 떵떵 쳤습니다.

참 이상해요.

사람 변하기로 치면 순식간이데요.

남편은 평생 누구 앞에서 흰소리를 하거나, 거짓말을 하거나, 공치사를 하는 사람이 아니었습니다. 그렇지만 독사 아가리보다 무서운 게 그놈의 돈바람이더라구요. 골프장 직원들 승용차에 실려 수시로 읍내를 들락거리면서, 남편은 하루가 다르게 달라졌습니다. 술에 취해, 여자들 향수 냄새를 잔뜩 묻혀 오는 날도 하루 이틀이 아니었지요. 골프장 직원이 오면, 무슨 비밀 이야기가 그리도 많은지, 대청마루 놔두고 직원이 타고 온 차에 들어가 밀담을 나누곤 했습니다.

안 좋은 소문이 많아, 신랑 단속 잘해.

경훈 오빠가 짐짓 내게 말한 적도 여러 번 있었습니다.

worst winds of urban development, but I still believe. I believe the elders who say the good water is why we had such devoted, filial children, why the people are so generous and kind. Most of the human body is water, you know. Imagine a body always full of clear, fragrant water. It would just naturally purify the soul, don't you think?

I suppose I ought to go back to talking about that day.

Yes, I ought to tell you what happened that day that I went to the prison. You see, Foreman Suh didn't actually come back home the day he was supposed to be released. His younger brother, who'd gone to meet him, came back alone, saying there'd been a mistake with the paperwork, that we'd all had the wrong day. Foreman Suh's real release date was actually one day later than the day we'd been told. Like a man awaiting the fast approach of some fateful ruination, my husband had been guarding our home all day long. But then, around nightfall, he received a phone call and dressed himself to go out.

I'm going to go see about something.

He almost sounded as if he was talking to him-

어느 편이냐 하면, 대세를 돌이킬 수 없다고 생각하긴 했으나 경훈 오빠는 골프장 건설을 애초 반대한 사람 중 한 명이었어요. 우리 동네가 마지막 마을인데, 안쪽 지대 높은 곳에 골프장이 생기면 마을 앞을 흘러가는 계곡물도 시궁창물이 될 것이고, 골프장 잔디밭에 뿌릴 독한 농약을 핥고 내려온 물로 논밭 망치기 쉬우며, 무엇보다 커가는 아이들은 물론 여자들 버리기 십상이라는 것이었습니다. 캐디인가 뭔가, 그 여자들 행실이 영 글렀다는 게야, 경훈 오빠는 그런 말도 했습니다. 당연지사, 남편과 그 사람 사이는 급격히 벌어지기 시작했지요. 자네가 뭘 안다고, 라고 남편은 말했습니다. 우리 집 마당의 평상에 몇몇 사람이 앉아 술 한 잔 나누고 있던 저녁이었어요. 거나하게 취한 남편이 얼마 전 골프장 직원이 놓고 간 양주를 꺼내 와서 한바탕 자랑을 늘어놓은 게 화근이었습니다. 시버스 리갈이라죠. 예전 박 대통령이 시해될 때 마시던 술 말예요. 비윗장이 상한 경훈 오빠가, 요즘 서울 사람들은 시버스 리갈, 그런 거, 싸구려라고 안 마신답디다, 어깃장을 놓았습니다. 양주 몇 병에 돈 많은 놈들 밑씻개를 자원할 거냐고 한, 경훈 오빠의 말은 내가 듣기에도 좀 심했습니다. 감히

self.

Even as he told me that he might not be back until the following night, that I shouldn't wait up for him, my husband wouldn't look at me. His eyes were sunken into his face, the skin around them dark. The whites were bloodshot, and his pupils were uneasy, flitting from side to side as if they were searching for something. We hadn't said a word to one another since the night before. I knew I should ask him where he was going, but somehow the words wouldn't leave my lips, and my ears were still ringing, echoing with his final words from the night before: I should have known something was going on from the moment you said you wanted to move here... He took a long, long time tying his shoelaces, and I just sat there, mute, watching him. It was night, but the temperature still hadn't gone down; it was so hot the air itself felt like a pressure cooker.

When he was almost at the front gate, my husband turned and walked back over to the shed.

That's when I saw it. What my husband was carrying when he came back out of the shed. It was the blade of the scythe he had been sharpening the night before, the one that had been sitting out in

이놈이 얻다 대고, 남편이 술상을 마당으로 홱 팽개친 건 순식간의 일이었어요. 상을 마당으로 팽개치다니요. 재판장님, 단언하지만 남편은 본래 그런 사람이 아니었습니다. 회사가 부도나서 쫓겨 다닐 때에도, 더 높은 사람은 이리저리 다 빠져나가고 남편이 애꿎게 옥살이를 할 때에도, 누구 한번 대놓고 욕하는 소리조차 내지 않던, 내 남편 홍이섭 씨는 본래 그런 사람입니다.

여보, 숙이 아빠.

고개 들고 나 좀 봐요.

법정에서, 법 없이 열 번 생을 다시 살아도 살 당신, 당신과 내가, 이 치욕적인, 더러운 심문을 박치기로 주고받으며, 마주보고 서서, 이게 뭐예요, 대체. 어쩌다 이 지경이 된 거냐구요. 내가 공주교도소로 갈 거, 당신은 뻔히 알고 있었어요. 그래서 날 뒤따라왔겠지만요. 함정을 파 놓고, 그게 당신 머리에서만 나왔다곤 믿지 않지만, 어떻게 나를, 우리 모든 것까지 엮어서, 세상에, 어떻게 어떻게 그런, 날 좀 봐요, 여보. 나를, 더러운, 우리를 좀 보라구요, 제발.

죄송합니다.

예, 주의하겠습니다, 재판장님.

the middle of the yard. Taken out of the shed. Not the scythe itself, but the blade. Who knew when he'd done it, but the blade had been separated from the handle at some point; it was just a naked blade, now. The part of the blade that had been embedded in the handle was wound round and round with tape, so you could grip it. My husband wrapped the whole thing in a towel and stuffed it into his back pocket, and then he left. It was as if he wanted me to see, to know.

Of course I couldn't sleep.

It was a long, sweltering, frightening night.

I got on the first bus into town, and it was only around nine thirty in the morning when I reached the front gate of the Gongju Correctional Institute. The guard told me that released prisoners would be coming out a little after ten. I just naturally assumed that Foreman Suh's younger brother would be coming to meet him as well. But ten o'clock came and went and not a single glimpse of that familiar face. It was maybe ten after ten or so. The big metal gates opened, and the small waiting crowd, with their tofu and their gourds, milled in closer and closer, and then, out he came. He was wearing a shirt plastered with the golf course logo.

갑자기 복받쳐서요. 그, 그러지요. 재판장님만을 바라보고 말하겠습니다. 그동안의 일들은 재판장님도 대강 파악하셨으리라 믿고 긴 말 하지 않을게요. 남편과 서이장님 사이엔 이번 일 말고도 여러 건의 고소 고발 사건이 아직 미결인 채 남아 있습니다. 남편을 폭행해서서 이장님이 옥살이하고 나온 건 모두 아는 일이지요. 하지만 그것도 따져보면 그렇습니다. 현장엔 골프장 총무부장하고 직원하고 당사자들밖에 없었어요. 보지 않았으나 손바닥처럼 그림이 눈에 뵙니다. 벌써 삼 년 이상 겪어 왔는데 골프장 측 노는 방법, 내가 왜 모르겠습니까. 간단히 말해서 골프장 측이 우리 동네를 다루는 방법은 두 가지뿐이라구요. 상상력이 젬병이에요. 삼 년 전 써먹은 수법을, 이십 년 전 삼십 년 전 기업들이 써먹은 수법을 아직도 고스란히 전수받아 써먹고들 있다구요.

세상 달라졌다는 말 나는 믿지 못합니다.

민주화, 새천년, 인터넷, 모두 웃기는 얘기예요. 달라진 건 겉옷뿐이지요. 상생이라고 하던가요. 너 죽고 나 살자 하지 말고, 너 죽고 나 죽고 하지 말고, 너 살고 나도 살아 상생, 예전엔 더불어, 라고 했던 말, 공동체, 라

To think that I'd be seeing that mark again, and there, of all places.

My husband was Village Foreman, back when those shirts first came out. I know you've heard this already, Your Honor, but our village holds open elections for Foreman every two years; there are no limits on reelection. Before Foreman Suh eventually won out over him by a single vote, my husband had been reelected twice, making it a total of three two-year terms. He had experience accounting, after all, and he was known to be detail-oriented, and fair. Everyone said he was made for the job. In fact, if it weren't for the golf course, my husband would probably still be our Foreman.

I know you know all this, Your Honor, but please, let me say my piece.

As was often the case, when the golf course was first announced, opinions were split among the villagers. Before they even started any construction, a representative for the golf course had donated some thirty million *won* to the village fund, and that really seemed like a whole lot of money to those country folk. Some wanted to split the money evenly between all the different households, and some wanted to leave it untouched, in the fund.

고 했던 말, 이제 민주화 세계화했으니, 보통 사람도 제각각 제몫몫, 말할 거 말하고 요구할 거 요구하게 됐으니, 옳거니, 새 세상에 맞추어야지, 얼른 얼른 새로운 말 덮어씌워 상생, 서로 상(相) 날 생(生) 상생, 하고 보면 우리 사는 세상, 가야 할 방향으로 잘 가고 있구나, 모두들 제 빛깔로, 억울할 거 없는 제몫의 삶을 살고 있다고 느끼지만요, 개뿔이나, 겉옷을 바꿔 입었을 뿐이라는 거, 나는 알아요. 나무양판이 쇠양판되남요?

첫째는 돈입니다, 도온.

현찰을 만지면 너나없이 판단이 흐려지고 속된 말로 맛이 간다는 거, 골프장은 잘 알고 있습니다. 삼천만 원 한꺼번에 배팅하고, 이렇게 저렇게 노임이다 뭐다 푼돈 풀어주자 골프장 건설 반대의견이 용두사미로 주저앉았다는 건 아까 말씀드렸지요. 이층짜리 마을회관도 지어줬습니다. 공돈인 거 같아 보이지만 천만의 말씀이에요. 우리 모두 칠팔십 년대, 지겹게 경험한 거지요. 삼천만 원을 미쳤다고 골프장에서 공으로 줍니까. 비록 남은 자재로 남은 인력 동원해서 지어줬다지만 마을회관 괜히 기증합니까. 몇 배씩 다른 이득을 계산하고 하는, 일테면 낚싯밥인 셈인데요, 뻔한, 상상력 없는 그 수법

There were a few people who were against the construction from the very start, but when that thirty million came in their protests grew vague, and the focus of the argument shifted to what we should do with the money. The people at the golf course assured everyone that once the construction was over, they would pay us more. The whole village started buzzing at that. One young housewife announced she was going to get a job as a caddie. Once the construction started, every last farm worker left the fields for the building site. The pay was much better there, you see. It all just spread in a flash, like a forest fire on a windy day.

Once the construction was in full swing, with the trucks coming in and out and the mountain coming down, the dirt and dust got so bad you couldn't even hang your laundry out to dry. But even then no one had any complaints. See, all that time, every house in village was getting a few crisp ten thousand *won* bills a day. It might not seem like much to someone living in a city, but when you're in remote little Jeongsu-ri, when your family has been farming peppers, or maybe tobacco, for generation after generation—well, then you're used to two adults in one household working the fields all day

이 전가의 보도라, 삼십 년 전이나 지금이나 여전히 효과만점이라 그 말입니다. 마을회관을 지어주면서 동시에 공동수도를 놔주겠다고 했어요. 공동수도 말예요. 집집마다 수도관을 부엌까지 놔주겠다고 나온 거지요. 남편이 사람들을 모아 놓고 설득합디다. 우리가 먹는 우물물은 겨우 십여 미터 땅 파서 퍼 올리는 물이지만, 마을 공동수도를 설치하면 지하 백 미터, 백오십 미터에서 퍼 올리니 그야말로 약수 중 약수라는 것이었어요. 그때까지 왜 골프장 측에서 공동수도를 놔주겠다는 것인지, 그 속셈은 아무도 몰랐습니다. 남편만은 알고 있었을까요.

대학부설 전문 연구기관에 의뢰한 바……

남편은 소리쳐 또 말했습니다.

우물물의 수질검사 결과가 불안정하게 나왔다고 했습니다. 피피엠이라는 알아듣기 힘든 용어도 등장했구요. 골프장 총무부장이 서류봉투를 단정히 무릎에 올려놓은 채 눈을 지그시 감고 앉아 남편의 열렬한 설명을 심각하게 듣고 있었습니다. 마을 사람의 삼분지 이 정도는 이미 우물에 모터펌프를 달아 자가수도를 부엌까지 설치해 쓰고 있었으니 특별히 불편할 정도는 아니었

to bring in, say, a hundred thousand in cash, combined. Whether you were initially against the construction or not, living like that, how could you just turn down all that easy money?

And on top of all this, the golf course had decided that anyone from our little area, even elders over sixty, would get special consideration—a full five hundred thousand *won* per day for any work they did on site. What kind of construction work could an elder over sixty really do? They would just go on out and go through the motions and just bring on home fifty thousand *won* for the day. The golf course was just handling us, the people of Jeongsu-ri, the only village around, petting and cajoling and pleasing us as well as they could. As for my husband, he went around bragging, blustering that it was all thanks to him, the Foreman, it was all because of him that even the elders were getting the chance to work for that kind of pay.

It's so strange, really.

As it turns out, a person can change in no more than an instant. His whole life, my husband had never been the kind of man to brag, or lie, or flatter. But you know what's scarier than a poisonous snake? Money. Before long he was getting rides to

습니다. 그래서 슬쩍 수질검사 얘기를 흘린 것이지요. 누군가가, 우리 동네 우물물이 못 먹게 됐단 말이냐고 물었습니다. 그게 아, 아니구요, 라고 남편이 골프장 총무부장을 슬쩍 곁눈질해 보고 대답했습니다. 현재는 그런대로 먹을 만하지만 앞으로 오염될 가능성이 크다는 얘깁니다. 남편은 그 말끝에 읍내 서쪽에 새로 조성된 염색공단을 쳐들고 나왔습니다. 전문가들의 견해에 따르면 지하수가 그쪽 방향에서 동네 쪽으로 흐르고 있으니 얕은 우물물이 오염될 건 시간문제라는 것이었습니다. 하기야 오염이 되든 안 되든, 공동수도를 굳이 놔준다는 데 반대할 사람은 아무도 없었습니다.

수도공사는 곧장 시작됐습니다.

읍내로 나가는 북쪽만 약간 열린 듯할 뿐, 우리 정수리는 삼태기 같은 형세의 연접된 산자락에 쏙 들어앉아 있습니다. 동쪽 산자락 여기저기에 지하수 개발을 위한 시설물이 이내 설치됐지요. 자연생 잣나무들이 쭉쭉 뻗어 올라간 산자락으로, 그 너머에 위치한 골프장과 가장 가까운 곳이었습니다.

아따, 물공이를 왜 저렇게 여러 군데 파나.

어떤 사람은 고개를 갸웃하고 말했습니다.

and from the village in the sedan cars of those golf course people, and he just started changing, one day to the next. It wasn't just once or twice that he came home late at night, drunk and smelling of perfume. And whenever someone from the golf course stopped by, instead of just coming in and sitting in the living room, they would sit out in the employee's car. All I'm saying is, who on earth has so many secrets?

There are a lot of bad rumors going around; keep an eye on that man of yours, Gyeong-hun *Oppa* took care to warn me. And it happened more than once.

As for Gyeong-hun *Oppa* himself, well, he understood that there was no way to turn back the clock, but he'd started out on the side that was against the golf course from the very beginning. Our village had always been the last one on the road, and he pointed out that once the golf course came in and built on the high ground, sewage from the construction site would dirty the creek that flowed through our village, The pesticides they sprayed on the grass could easily seep into the water and pollute our fields, and that, more than anything, it would be a bad influence on the wom-

조립식 패널 지붕을 한 가건물 안에 대형 물탱크가 들어가 앉았고, 골목길이며 집 안이며, 수도관을 묻는 공사가 일사천리로 진행됐습니다. 새로운 소문이 돌기 시작한 것은 집 안의 공사가 거의 마무리될 때쯤이었지요. 골프장이 있는 곳에선 지하수가 안 나온다, 여러 군데 파 보았으나 얼마 안 가 물이 말랐다, 이 근처에서 지하수가 풍부한 곳은 우리 동네뿐이다, 골프장에서 쓸 물을 여기서 끌어가려는 것이다, 소문을 요약하자면 대강 이랬습니다. 마을회관에 사람들이 다시 모였습니다. 골프장 물을 전부 여기서 가져다 쓴다는 소문은 잘못된 것입니다, 라고 총무부장이 설명했지요. 골프장 부지 안에서 이미 우물을 여러 군데 팠고, 그중의 일부에선 물이 잘 나오고 있다 했습니다. 다만 그것으로 충분하지 않을 것에 대비해 마을 수도공사를 하며, 몇 개의 지하수 심정을 박고 송수관 설치를 했으니 양해해달라는 말이었지요. 지하수는 마르지 않으니 걱정하실 것 없습니다. 총무부장은 느릿느릿 말했습니다.

말라붙으면 어떻게 합니까.

더 깊이 파면 되지요.

누군가 묻자 총무부장은 간단히 대답했고, 심드렁한

en and younger children. These women who called themselves caddies, Gyeong-hun *Oppa* thought their morals were questionable at best. That's what he said.

As you might imagine, his friendship with my husband suffered; they grew apart, and fast. You don't know anything, is what my husband told him. It was evening, and a handful of people were sitting around our front deck area, having a drink. It had all started when my husband, roaring drunk, brought out a bottle of scotch someone from the golf course had given him as a gift and set to bragging. Chivas Regal, they call it. The same thing President Park was drinking when he was assassinated.

Disgusted, Gyeong-hun *Oppa* began to provoke him, saying, These days, no one in Seoul drinks Chivas Regal—they think it's cheap booze. What, are you so used to kissing their asses for a couple bottles of cheap booze that you're going to start wiping their asses next?

Gyeong-hun *Oppa* went a bit far there, even I'll admit that. How dare you! Who do you think you are! And with that, my husband upended the table into the yard.

총무부장의 태도 때문에 긴장이 풀린 사람들이 잡담을 시작했습니다. 여러분에게 위로금을 더 지급할 예정입니다, 라고 총무부장이 때맞추어 낚싯밥을 매달았지요. 마을 이장에게 위임하여 대표 몇 사람을 뽑아주면 그들과 협의하겠다는 것이었습니다. 남편이 그 다음 일어났습니다. 난 이 문제로 읍내에 나가 변호사도 만나고 왔습니다, 라고 남편이 말하자 잡담소리가 뚝 끊겼습니다.

우리는 공동수도를 사용해 온 게 아니에요.

남편이 말했습니다.

총무부장이 슬그머니 자리를 뜬 뒤의 일입니다. 짜 맞춘 듯 그들은 바통 터치를 한 거지요. 법적으로는, 각자 집 안에 독립적으로 자가수도나 우물을 사용해 왔을 경우, 토지소유권에 의해 지하수를 사용해 왔을 뿐이므로, 지하수 사용권을 마을이 총유(總有)한 걸로 보지 않는다는 설명이었습니다. 법적으로는 적어도 그렇다고 했습니다. 항차 법적으로 그러할진대, 우리가 쓰고 마시는 데 부족함이 없다면 인정으로라도 이웃과 나눠 써야 할 것이고, 더구나 나눠주는 값으로 실리를 거둘 수 있으면 금상첨화라, 반대할 이유가 전혀 없다는 얘기였습니다. 사람들은 당연지사 고개를 끄덕일밖에요. 서

Your Honor, I can assure you, my husband was not the kind of man who would do something like that. To flip a table full of bottles and glasses into the yard! Even when his company went bankrupt and we had to go into hiding, even when his higher ups got away clean and he still had to finish out his prison term, even then I never once heard him say a bad word about anyone—that's the kind of man he used to be. That was my husband, Hong Yi-seop.

Darling. Honey.

Look up here. Raise your head and look at me, honey.

What are we doing here in this courtroom, what are we doing here, when I'd be with you again, another ten lives over and ovcr again, no matter the law? What are we doing, you and me, forcing each other to submit to these degrading, dirty interrogations, standing across from one another—what is this? How did we get here? You knew—you knew better than anyone that I would go to Gongju, to the prison. That's why you followed me. You set a trap, and I know, I know there's no way you thought it all up yourself, but still, how could you? To me? How could you drag all our—look at me,

이장님과 몇몇 사람들이 이의를 제기한 것도 사실이지만 주장은 미미했습니다. 곧 몇몇 대표자를 남편이 지명했고, 얼마 후, 오천만 원의 보상금이 지급될 거라는 소문이 돌았습니다. 불과 서른일곱 가구가 사는 마을입니다. 가구당 나눠 가져도 백만 원이 넘는 돈이었지요.

사건은 그렇게 생겨난 것입니다.

아니에요, 재판장님. 이번 사건과 그 일이 별 상관없다는 말씀엔 동의할 수 없습니다. 모든 싸움의 원천은 거기에 있어요. 우리 동네가 그 후로 어떻게 됐는지, 동네 사람들이 모두 무엇을 하고 어떤 모습으로들 살아가고 있는지 재판장님도 아셔야 합니다. 간통이 뭐 그리 큰 문제입니까.

단언하지만, 우리 집 그이, 간통에 관심 없으리라고 봅니다.

이게 어디, 간통을 두고 하는 싸움인가요? 다들 몇 년 사이, 무엇이 옳고 그른지, 무엇을 지키고 무엇을 버려야 할지 깡그리 잊어버렸습니다. 예전의 우리 동네라면 간통이 큰 문제였겠지만요, 지금은 아니라구요. 동네 어르신네들한테 한번 물어보세요. 소주 한잔 하는데도 꼭 자가용 몰고 읍내나 서울로 나가는 세상이 됐습니

darling—look at your wife. Look at me, at us, at this awful—Look at us, I'm begging you.

I'm sorry, Your Honor.

Yes, I'll remember, Your Honor.

It just came over me all of a sudden. Yes, sir, I will. I'll just keep my eyes on you, Your Honor. I'll trust that you have a general understanding of what went on after that, and try to keep things short. I'll just say that my husband and Foreman Suh are embroiled in a number of open court cases against one another in addition to this one. Everyone here already knows that Foreman Suh did prison time for beating up my husband. But you know, even that isn't as straightforward as you might think. Other than the two of them, no one actually saw what happened except the general manager of the golf course and another employee. I may not have been there myself, but I can easily guess how it went. I've been living with it for three years—how could I not know how those golf course people like to entertain themselves?

To put it simply, the golf course only has two ways of dealing with us villagers. They have zero imagination. They're still using the same tactics they did three years before, the same rotten tactics cor-

다. 불과 삼 년 만의 일입니다. 재판장님. 골프장으로 일 나가다가 바람 든 부인 때문에 풍비박산 난 집도 있고, 형제간에 돈 놓고 맞고소한 집안도 있어요. 토요일 일요일마다 일손을 돕겠다고 고향집으로 돌아오곤 하던 젊은 자식들도 이젠 없습니다. 부모가 농사를 안 짓는데 뭐하러 일손을 도우러 옵니까. 지금 대처에 살던 자식들이 돌아오면 어르신네들은 공포감으로 도망가고 싶다고 하십니다. 돌아오는 자식마다 너나없이 늙은 부모들한테 오히려 손을 벌리니까요. 농사를 짓지 않고 버려진 논밭들엔 잡초만 무성하고, 동네로 들어오는 길목엔 생기느니 가든과 여관뿐입니다. 다 골프장 손님들의 수요에 따라 생기는 것이지요. 사람들은 잔뜩 독이 올라 걸핏하면 멱살잡이를 합니다. 남편은 서 이장을 폭행, 무고, 협박, 명예훼손으로 고소했고, 서 이장은 남편을 역시 폭행, 무고에 공문서 위조, 사기 등으로 고소했습니다. 어디 남편과 서 이장뿐인 줄 아십니까. 고소고발 사건의 재판이 동네 사람끼리 지금 진행되고 있는 것만도 네 건이나 된다구요. 삼사 년 사이 모모한 동네 사람들, 거의 변호사 수준이 됐어요. 한 건이 끝나면 또 다른 건으로 고소하고, 또 다른 건이 불리해지면 새로

porations they've been passing down and using for the last thirty years. They say the world has changed, but I don't believe it. Democratization, the new millennium, the internet—it's all a joke to me. The only thing that's changed is the outer garment.

They call it "*sang-saeng*," don't they? Cohabitation. It's not you die and I die, and it's not you die and I live, it's you live and I live, too. It's everyone living together. We used to call it communal living, but now, in this age of democracy and globalization, now that even ordinary folks can look out for their own best interests, now that everyone can say what they have to say and demand what they want to demand, well, we have to adapt to this new reality, to evolve with the times. "*Sang*" for one another, "*saeng*" for life; thinking about it it feels like this world we're living in isn't so bad, that we're all going in the right direction, each of us getting to be our own hue, each of us in charge of our own destiny. What garbage. The only thing that's changed is the outer garment, like I said. Wood doesn't just turn into metal, you know?

First and foremost comes money. Money.

They say if you touch a lot of cash it starts to blur your judgment, makes you lose your sense of

운 사단을 만들어 냅니다. 저기 두 양반, 아마 죽을 때까지 경찰서다 법원이다 드나들며 살게 될 거라고 봐요. 서 이장 이장 당선 원인무효소송이 끝난 지 불과 한 달밖에 안됐습니다. 곧 있을 이장 선거에 남편은 또 출마하겠지요. 와신상담, 기다려 왔으니까요. 남편파, 서 이장파, 원수지간도 세상에, 이런 원수지간이 없다구요. 어디 남편파 서 이장파뿐인 줄 아세요. 징그럽습니다. 끔찍합니다. 피의자는 최후진술을 할 권리가 있다고 들었어요.

그러니 내 말을, 재판장님일지라도 더 이상 막지 마시라구요.

내가 좀 흥분했군요. 죄송합니다.

요컨대, 이야기는 다시 우물입니다.

공동수도 공사가 끝난 게 가을이었고요, 이듬해 봄에 골프장을 개장했습니다. 때맞추어 읍내에서 들어오는 십 리 길이 이차선 포장도로로 깨끗이 단장됐지요. 빠져나갈 데 없는 외통수 길인데, 관에서 하는 도로 확장 공사가 골프장 개장에 맞춰 이루어진 것도 참 의미심장한 일이라고 생각해요. 어쨌든 봄이 왔고, 사람들은 파

things; no one knows the truth of that better than those folks at the golf course. When they handed over that thirty million *won* all at once, and then all those little sums of cash, this and that, the day wages for the elders—well, like I said before, it just wiped out all opposition.

They even built us a two-story village hall. It was supposed to be public, of course, but it was nothing of the kind. It's the same old thing we all got so used to, back in the seventies and eighties. After all, why would the golf course hand over thirty million *won* for nothing? What are they, crazy? Sure, they said that they built it with the leftover funds and with leftover manpower, but then why would they donate a village hall for free? They were calculating it all along, the profits they would make. It was bait, in other words.

And it all just proves that the same exact methods, the same obvious, unimaginative tricks are still every bit as effective as they were thirty years ago. They said that since they were already building the hall, they would just go ahead and lay public water pipes for the whole village. Public water pipes. They were going to lay pipes for each house, so we could all have running water in our kitchens. My

종 준비를 하고 모판을 만들었어요. 몇몇 재래식 우물이 말라버렸다는 걸 알았지만 공동수도를 통해 집집마다 물이 콸콸 쏟아졌으므로 별로 신경 쓰는 사람은 없었습니다. 내가 어린 시절을 보냈던 친정집 우물도, 새로 판 우리 집 뒤뜰의 우물도 뿌연 물이 바닥을 간신히 가리고 있을 뿐이었어요.

어떡한데.

한숨을 쉬고 내가 말했습니다.

검은 옷을 입은 밤이 이제 어디로 숨나.

바보 같은 소리 좀 그만해, 라고 남편이 꽥 소리를 지르데요. 일 년 전의 남편이었다면 나의 그런 소녀 같은 말에, 역시 우리 마누라는 시인이야, 대꾸했을 텐데 남편은 한심하다는 듯 혀까지 차고 돌아섰습니다. 어디로 옮겨가 숨었든, 밤은 어김없이 찾아왔습니다. 그런데 참 이상한 일이더라구요. 가로등까지 밝은데요, 골프장에 설치된 나이트 시설이 켜지기라도 하는 날엔 사철나무 밑동까지 훤해지는데요, 밤이, 어둠이요, 예전과 달리 무서워지기 시작했습니다. 아무리 캄캄해도 예전의 정수리에선 무섭지가 않았어요. 낮엔 축축한 검은 옷을 입은 채 우물 밑에 숨어 있다가 저물녘이면 슬그머니

husband gathered all villagers together to win them over to the cause. He said that the well water we all drank was coming from maybe ten meters down, no more, but if we could get a water system installed for the whole village, well, that water would be coming from at least a hundred, maybe even a hundred and fifty meter deep, and that, he assured everyone, would be the best water of all. At that point no one had any idea about the real reason the golf course was offering to do this for us. I wonder if my husband knew.

We've spoken with the fine folks at the university research institute... He was practically yelling, that husband of mine.

He said they had run tests, that the water quality of our wells had come out as unstable. He used obscure terms like 'PPM.' The golf course manager just sat there, eyes closed, a thick envelope resting on his lap, listening solemnly as my husband put forth his impassioned arguments. Almost a third of the villagers had already installed motorized pumps in their wells, so many people already had running water in their kitchens. There was no great discomfort.

That's why they spread all that talk about the wa-

사철나무 그늘로 나와 앉아, 어둠의 커다란 물레를 돌린다는, 그리하여 온 천지에 연기 풀 듯, 어둠을 풀어낸다는 그 키 큰 아저씨, 밤이 친구 같았으니까요. 그런데 밤은 더 이상 친구가 아니었어요. 여중학교 일 학년 애가 막 버스를 놓쳐 동네까지 걸어오다가 몹쓸 사람한테 걸려 성폭행을 당한 사건도 그해 봄의 일이었습니다. 저녁이면 뒤뜰을 나가는 것도 그렇게 무섭더라구요, 머리털이 쭈뼛 서고요.

심각한 문제는 논에서 생겼습니다.

모내기를 하려고 며칠이나 고생해 물을 담아두었는데, 막상 모내기를 하려고 나가보니 논물이 온데간데없는 일이 생겨났어요. 뱀장어나 웅지 따위가 논둑의 구멍을 낸 흔적도 없고, 다른 집 논으로 물이 흘러간 자국도 없으니 귀신 곡할 노릇일밖에요. 철렁하게 담아둔 논물이, 세상천지, 하룻밤 새 어디로 사라진단 말입니까. 처음에야 고개 갸웃갸웃하면서, 그래도 어쨌든, 모내기들을 하고 계곡물을 잡아넣고 했는데요. 머잖아 밑 빠진 독에 물 붓기라는 걸 사람들은 알아차렸습니다. 지하수를 하도 퍼내니까 지상은 손쉽게 물들이 말라버리는 거지요. 비가 내려도 물이 고여 있는 건 며칠뿐이

ter quality tests. Someone asked if anyone in the village had actually had to stop drinking their well water.

That's—that's not the point, is how my husband replied, his eyes flitting toward the general manager. The water is potable so far, more or less, but what we're saying is that there's a high risk of contamination in the future.

And with that, he brought up the dye factory that had just been built to the west of the village. The experts, he said, thought that because the groundwater flowed from that direction toward the village, it was only a matter of time before any water close to the surface became contaminated. And really, contamination or no contamination, who would refuse an offer to have water pipes put in for them for free? No one.

The construction for the pipes began right away.

Other than the northern edge of the village, the way out to town, our little village of Jeongsu-ri is basically closed in on three sides, nestled right up against the mountain slopes. Before long, these structures were erected all along the eastern foothills to tap into the groundwater. It was close to the golf course, past the wild pine nut trees that

었어요. 그제야 사람들은 골프장에서 퍼 가는 지하수에 대해 구체적으로 묻기 시작했고, 새로 심은 잔디를 오뉴월의 뙤약볕에 말려 죽이지 않으려면 엄청난 양의 물이 필요하다는 걸 알게 됐습니다. 가증스럽게도 골프장은 필요한 물의 전량을 우리 동네에서 퍼 가고 있었습니다. 골프장 일대에 심정을 박아 지하수를 개발하려고 애쓴 건 사실이었으나, 실패했던 거지요. 근동에서 지하수가 풍부한 곳은 불행히도 우리 동네 일대밖엔 없었어요.

한 달이면 칠백 톤 이상의 물이 골프장에 필요하다고 했습니다.

설상가상, 골프장 구내에 사원들 연수를 한답시고 콘도미니엄을 짓기 시작했으니, 그게 완성되면 물은 더욱 필요해지겠지요. 달마다 커다란 호수가 통째로 골프장으로 빨려 올라가는 꼴이에요. 게다가 잔디를 유지하기 위한 농약이 하도 독하게 섞여서, 골프장을 지나 내려오는 계곡수는 쓸모가 없었습니다. 가을이 되기 전에 벼는 누렇게 단풍이 들었고 사람들은 농사일을 포기하고 말았습니다. 무리지어 골프장에 쫓아 올라가 항의도 하고 보상도 요구했지만 그들은 여유만만이었어요. 보

grow along those slopes.

By God, why are they digging in so many places? Someone or other pointed out, cocking their heads to one side.

They erected a building with a temporary panel roof and put a huge water tank inside it and the water pipe construction progressed with lightning speed in every alley, every home.

A new batch of rumors started circulating right around when all the in-house construction was wrapping up. In sum, people were basically saying that there was no groundwater over by the golf course, that they kept digging new wells and the wells kept drying up, that the only place around there with good water was our little area, that they were planning on getting the water for the golf course from our village. Everyone gathered at the village hall once more.

It's just not true that we're planning on taking all the water for the golf course from here, the general manager explained. He said that they had already dug quite a few wells over on the golf course itself, and that several of them were giving excellent water. He said that the water pipe construction was just a contingency, in case the well water wasn't

상할 건 이미 다 했다는 것이고, 주민들 모두의 동의서도 받아 두었으니 법적으로도 전혀 책임이 없다는 얘기였습니다. 골프장에서 보여준 서류 중엔 마을 사람 모두가 앞으로 영원히, 무제한으로, 마을 지역 내의 지하수를 골프장 측이 사용해도 이의를 제기하지 않겠다는 동의서가 인감도장까지 찍힌 채로 첨부되어 있었습니다. 그 동의서의 대가로 마을 사람이 받은 건 가구당 약 백삼십만 원씩 이미 나누어 가진, 오천만 원이었습니다. 사람들은 남편과 남편이 지명한 몇몇 대표자들을 찾아다니며 악을 썼지요. 그래도 결과는 마찬가지였습니다. 대표자들과 남편에게 위임한다면서 인감도장을 내준 것은 그들 자신이었으니까요. 당신이 골프장에서 쓸 물의 일부만 우리 동네에서 가져간다고 했잖소, 라고 말하면서 이장 동생이 총무부장의 멱살을 움켜잡았습니다. 총무부장은 미소 지으며 대꾸했습니다.

아, 골프장에서 물이 나온다면야 그랬겠죠.

서 이장 동생은 너무 화가 난 나머지 총무부장의 따귀를 갈겼고, 한 시간도 안돼 읍내에서 나온 경찰차가 폭행죄라면서 그를 데려갔습니다. 남편과 서 이장이 처음으로 치고 박고 싸운 게 그날 저녁의 일입니다. 남편

enough, that they could only ask for our understanding and patience. They had already installed several deep-well pumps for the water main. The groundwater would not dry up. There was no cause for concern. The general manager's speech was slow, measured.

What will you do if it does dry up?

We'll dig deeper.

That was the general manager's simple answer to that particular question. Something about his lackadaisical attitude broke the tension, and people started chatting quietly with one another off to the side. That was when he tossed out some more bait: We will, of course, be compensating you for your added trouble. He was saying that if we just gave our Foreman power of attorney and chose a few representatives, he would work out the details of the agreement with them. That was when my husband stood up. I have been to town to meet with a lawyer, he announced, and the buzz of the side chatter stopped immediately.

The water we've had up to now has not been for common use. That's what my My husband said.

This was after the general manager had slipped out. It was as if they had handed off a baton. The

은 입술이 찢어졌고 서 이장은 코피가 터졌어요. 아무에게도 사전에 알릴 것 없이, 심지어 나한테도 말 한마디 없이, 골프장 쪽의 전화를 받고 나간 남편은 점심때 돌아와, 그 자식을 고발했어, 말했습니다. 골프장 쪽에서 서 이장을 폭행죄로 고발하고, 친절하게 차에 모시고 경찰서까지 데려간 결과였지요. 동생이 풀려나기도 전에 서 이장이 이번엔 연행됐고요, 그 다음날엔 서 이장의 맞고발로 남편도 경찰서로 불려갔습니다. 서로 피해자라고 주장하다가 피차 고발을 취하해 일단락된 그 첫 번째 폭행사건은 문제의 본질을 엉뚱한 쪽으로 몰고 가는 결정적인 계기가 됐습니다. 어쨌든 그 후부터 골프장과 맞서 싸워야 할 싸움이, 골프장 문턱에도 안 가고, 동네 안에서 패가 갈려 악쓰고 싸우기 시작했으니까 말예요. 나중엔 들은 얘기지만, 연행된 서 이장에게 맞고발하라고, 친절히 일러주고 도와준 형사는 진즉부터 동네에선 골프장 사람이라고 소문난 형사였습니다. 남편에게 서 이장을 폭행죄로 고발하라고 부추길 때, 이미 맞고발의 시나리오가 쓰여 있었던 거죠.

원리가 그렇습니다.

아주 고전적 방법이에요.

basic gist was that, legally, since we had all been using our own wells and pumps in our homes, this fell under the purview of private use of individual property, which meant, in turn, that the village did not collectively own the rights to the groundwater. Legally, he said, that's how things worked. But more important than any law, he went on, was the fact that if we had water to spare after using and drinking what we needed, we ought to be sharing with our neighbors anyway, if only out of decency, and, well, if this natural act of sharing was also compensated in practical terms, then that would just be that much better!

What was there to argue against that? The villagers, of course, all just nodded their heads. True, Foreman Suh and a couple of other people did raise some objections, but their protests were weak. And just like that, my husband named several village representatives then and there, and not long after, a rumor started going around that the village would be getting a fifty million *won* compensation check. The village only has thirty-seven households. Even if we split the funds between everyone, it would still have been over a million *won* per home.

현찰을 적당히 풀어 사람들 혼을 먼저 빼놓는 게 골프장의 첫 번째 방법이라면요, 아까 말씀 드렸다시피요, 두 번째 방법은요, 상상력 하나 없이 똑같이 써먹는, 지금은 물론 이십 년 전 삼십 년 전에도 돈 많고 힘 좋은 양반들이 쓰고 또 써먹어 온, 고전적, 상투적, 전통적인, 그러나 여전히 효과만점인 방법은요, 이쪽의 패를 갈리게 하는 것입니다. 이놈을 저놈이 의심하게 하고, 싫어하게 하고, 미워하게 하고, 또 저놈이 이놈을 의심, 혐오, 증오하게 한다 그 말이에요. 자중지란을 일으켜 놓으면 저희들끼리 미워하느라 애당초 문제의 본질이었던 것까지 깡그리 잊어버리거든요. 공부를 많이 못했습니다만, 역사적이라고 할까요, 영국이 아프리카를 잡아먹을 때에도, 미국이 인디언을 잡아먹을 때에도 그랬다더군요. 이쪽 종족에게 총을 줘서 저쪽 종족을 치게 하고, 원한에 사로잡힌 저쪽 종족에게 또 다른 총을 쥐어주며 원한을 갚으라 부추기는 것. 그러다보면 손 안 대고 코 푸는 식으로 저절로 싹쓸이되지 않겠냐구요.

요즘 우리 동네 현안은 이거예요.

작년에 새로 이장으로 선출된 서 이장님이 마을 대표자 자격으로 골프장에 소송을 걸었거든요. 마을 사람들

And that was the genesis of The Incident.

No, Your Honor. I'm afraid I don't agree that these things have no connection to the incident in question. These things make up the source of the entire conflict. You need to know, Your Honor, what happened to our village after that, and how our villagers are living, the state they're in now. I mean, how big a problem, really, is adultery? I can assure you, the man of my house is not the kind of person who cares deeply about something like adultery. What about this conflict is actually about adultery? Over just a few years, everyone's forgotten, somehow,—we've completely forgotten what's right and what's wrong, what we need to stand up for and what we need to let go. If this was our village here before all of this happened, adultery would have certainly been a huge issue. But not now. Ask any of the village elders. It's become the kind of life where you get in your car and drive out to town, or even to Seoul, just to have a drink of *soju*. That happened in just three years. Your Honor.

There are homes that have broken up because the wife got a job at the golf course and started an affair, and there are families where brothers are

이 내용을 잘 모르고 있는 상황에서 전 이장과, 그러니까 남편과 남편이 지명한 몇몇 대표자들이 임의로 동의서에 인감도장을 찍어주었으니까, 마을 지하수를 골프장에서 영구히 사용해도 좋다는 합의는 원천적으로 무효라는 거죠. 그러려면 다시 동의서를 받아야 한다, 영구히 지하수를 사용하는 값으로 최소한 십억 원을 지급하고 몇 년 간의 논농사 실패에 대해 따로 보상하라, 소송 내용은 이렇습니다.

일심법원 판결은 서 이장의 패소였습니다.

아까도 말했다시피, 지하수를 토지소유권대로 각각 집 안에서 단독적으로 사용해 왔으니까, 공동으로 그 권리를 가졌다고 볼 수 없다는 것이 법원의 판결 이유였고, 또 하나는 마을 이장은 법적 대표성에 문제가 있으니 사건을 각하하고 양측의 법정 비용은 소송을 제기한 서 이장이 물어야 한다는 것입니다.

사건은 당연지사, 상급법원으로 지금 가 있습니다.

만약 상급법원에서 판결이 뒤집어진다거나 하면 골프장도 곤란을 겪겠지만, 남편이나 남편을 도왔던 몇 사람은 아주 어려운 지경에 빠집니다. 왜냐하면 동의서를 위조한 것이 되니까요. 골프장도 그들의 피해를 남

actually suing each other over money. The sons and daughters who used to come back every Saturday and Sunday to help with the field work don't come home anymore either. Why would they, when their parents no longer farm? These days, the elders say they're scared of their children coming back to visit, that it makes them want to run away. Because, you see, now when these children come home every last one of them asks their aging parents for money.

The fields lie fallow, overgrown with weeds, and the road into town is riddled with restaurants and motels. They're all just meeting the demands of the golf course, of course. The people are different, ready to explode, grabbing at each other's collars over the slightest provocation. My husband has pressed charges against Foreman Suh for assault, false accusations, threats, and defamation, and Foreman Suh, in his turn, has pressed charges against my husband for assault, false accusations, counterfeiting government documents, and fraud. And don't think it's just the two of them. There are no fewer than four cases currently being tried, all villagers pitting themselves against one another. Just three, four years, and all these neighborly vil-

편에게 청구하는 소송을 제기할 거라고들 하데요. 사기죄도 될 수 있구요. 그러니까, 서 이장이 골프장을 상대로 한 지하수 사용 원천무효 소송은 사실은, 남편과 남편의 동조자들을 벼랑 끝으로 몰아가는 소송인데요, 그렇지만 승소냐 패소냐에 따라선, 서 이장 쪽도, 양측 소송비용까지 물어야 하니까, 그나마 얼마 안 되는 논밭까지 팔아 대야 할 처지가 됐습니다. 그야말로 피차 죽느냐 죽이느냐 판이 된 겁니다. 서 이장님이 남편을 곡괭이자루로 두들겨 패서 갈비뼈를 여러 대 부러뜨려 놓고 옥살이를 한 배경도 바로 그거예요. 골프장이야 설령 패소해도 손해배상을 청구할 데 있으니 느긋한 척 뒷짐지고 있는 판이구요. 힘을 합쳐도 내 곳간 지킬 둥 말 둥 한데, 골프장이 획책해 온 대로, 골프장의 대리전에, 결국 함께 죽는 그것. 앞으로 어느 누구도 감히 골프장에 덤빌 수 없도록 하려는 그 진부하고도 잔인한 원리. 평범한 아녀자도 아는 원리를 왜들, 아무도 모르는지 모르겠어요.

너무 장광설을 늘어놔 민망합니다.

내 변호사님이 눈짓을 보내시네요. 이쯤해서 결말로 가라는 뜻이겠지요. 혹은 내가 결심한 것들, 혹시 흔들

lagers, they've practically become lawyers themselves. When one case is closed they sue each other over something else. And if another case isn't going well, they come up with some new grievance.

Those two gentlemen sitting over there, I figure they'll both be in and out of police stations and courtrooms until the day they die. It's barely been a month since the case over Foreman Suh's election was declared baseless. Before long there will be another election, and I'm sure my husband will run again. He's been biding his time, you see, just waiting it out. My husband's camp, Foreman Suh's camp—I'm telling you, there have never been enemies like those two have been. And don't think it's just these two sides, either. It's just awful. I was told the accused always gets a chance to give their final testimony. So please, Your Honor, I know this is your courtroom, but please don't stop me anymore.

I got a little excited, didn't I. I apologize.

In sum, it all comes back to the well.

It was fall when the construction of the public water system was finally completed, and they

리지 않을까 걱정하시는지도 모르구요. 재판장님이나 방청객 여러분, 방청객이라야 대부분 우리 동네 어르신네들이지만요, 여러분이 기다리고 있는 게 어떤 이야기인지 압니다. 파라다이스로 가시죠, 그럼. 공주교도소에서 얼마 떨어지지 않은 곳에 있는 여관 이름이 파라다이스였어요. 아까 저쪽 변호사님이 예, 아니오로 대답하라며 이렇게 물으셨지요. 파라다이스 여관에 서 이장과 함께 들어간 게 사실이냐구요.

예, 사실입니다.

파라다이스 여관에 들어갔습니다.

출소한 사람 마중 나온 사람들이 거의 다 교도소 앞을 떠난 다음까지 서 이장님과 나는 너무나 많은 말들이 목젖에 걸려 아우성치는데, 그러나 한마디도 변변히 하지 못하고, 그 뜨거운 햇볕 아래 어색하게 서 있었습니다. 정말 무더운 날이었죠. 교도소 앞은 쨍쨍한 여름 햇볕에 부글부글 끓는 것 같았습니다. 나도 땀을 흘렸고, 그도 땀을 흘렸습니다. 몇 달 사이 서 이장님은 더욱 말랐고, 땀에 번질거리는 이마는 검붉었으며, 눈은 퀭한 것이 십 리쯤 들어가 있었습니다. 그는 어째서 내게 왜 공주까지 왔느냐고 묻지 않을까, 하고 처음엔 생각

opened the golf course the following spring. Just in time, the windy mountain path coming in from the village was redone, becoming a neat, paved, two-lane road. It's a dead end, that road, with no other way in or out; it's curious, don't you think, how the completion of this road construction, a public works project, just happened to coincide with the opening of the golf course?

But anyway, spring arrived, and everyone was preparing for the planting season and preparing their seedbeds. We all knew that a few of the conventional wells had dried up, but thanks to the new public water system, we all had running, gushing water in our homes, so no one had really given it much thought. Both the well at my old family house and the new well we had dug on our own land were drying up.—All that was left was a thin layer of murky water, just barely covering the bottom.

Oh dear.

Sighing, I turned to my husband:

Where will the night hide now, in its black clothes?

Stop talking nonsense! My husband shouted.

The husband I'd known just one year earlier

했고 시간이 지나며 그렇게 물어 올까 봐 겁이 났습니다.

내 안의 대답은 물론 확실했습니다.

무엇보다 내 남편을 구해야 한다고 생각했고, 또 그를 구해야 한다고 생각했습니다. 단번에 구하긴 부자가 천당 가는 것처럼 어렵겠지만, 남편이 잘 갈린 낫날을 품안에 넣고 살기 가득한 눈빛을 빛내며 집을 나설 때, 안 돼, 나는 부르짖었던 것입니다. 이대로 놔둘 수는 없어. 운명에 맡길 수 없어. 우선 막아야 돼. 막을 수 있는 방법이 무엇이든, 그 길만 있다면, 내가 설령 남편의 낫질을 당하고, 또 그의 동생이 사 놓았다는 엽총 세례를 받더라도 내가 갈 길을 갈 생각밖에 없었습니다. 그렇지만 그를 가로막고 서서, 내가 무슨 말을 꺼낼 수 있겠습니까. 우리 그이가 당신을 죽이려고 낫을 품고 있어, 라고 말해야 할까요. 아니면 차라리 나를 죽이라고, 나를 죽이지 않으려면 오늘 마을로 가지 말고 나랑 어디 먼 곳으로 가자고, 나를 좋아하지 않았었느냐고 말해야 할까요. 길고 참담하고 무거운 침묵을 깨뜨린 것은 결국 내가 아니라 그였습니다. 그가 목 언저리에 줄줄이 흐르는 땀을 한손으로 쓱 훔쳐 내고 나서 말했던 것입니다.

목간을 하고 싶어. 샤워를.

would have responded to the same girlish comment with a: Listen to that, my wife, the poet! But now, now he went so far as to cluck his tongue in disgust.

Night came, as usual, having found someplace else to hide, I suppose. But you know, it was very strange. Even though the streetlights were all burning bright, even though, sometimes, during the golf course's nighttime construction, even the ground under the spindle tree was lit up like it was the day, the darkness—it began to frighten me. The darkness was different, somehow. Before, I had never been frightened in Jeongsu-ri, no matter how dark it got. Because the night, the way it hid all day at the bottom of the well wearing its wet, black clothes, the way, when the sun went down, it crept out and sat under the spindle tree spinning its water wheel, spreading the darkness, like smoke, all across the world—that night, that gentleman, had felt almost like a friend. But now the night was no longer my friend. That same spring, some monster raped a seventh grader from the local girls' middle school, snatching her off the road after she missed her bus and had to walk home. It became frightening even to step out into the back

나는 교도소 안에 얼마나 좋은 샤워 시설이 있는지 잘 모릅니다. 암튼 그 말을 할 때의 그는 진짜 교도소에 가고 나서 단 한 번도 목간을 하지 않은 것처럼 보였습니다. 아침도 굶고, 뜬눈으로 지새우고, 여름 뙤약볕 밑에서 한 시간 이상 서 있던 나도 그에겐 그렇게 봤을는지 모르겠습니다만. 여관 층계를 올라갈 때, 붉은 카펫이 깔린 층계였는데요, 발소리가 전혀 나지 않는 것이 비로소 후둘후둘 떨리데요. 그는 문설주를 간신히 붙잡고 서 있는 내게 등을 보인 채, 정말 오로지 목욕을 하러 온 사람처럼, 훌렁훌렁 옷을 벗더니 욕실 안으로 들어갔습니다.

내가 그의 등에 비누칠을 해주었다구요?

아무렴요. 멋진, 영화에서 봤음직한 시나리옵니다. 또 그가 욕실 안에서 물 묻은 손으로 내 셔츠의 단추를 풀었단 말이지요? 요상한 그림이네요. 누가 쓴 시나리온지 알 수 없습니다. 그가 영화에서 본 대로 시나리오를 구상했을 수도 있고, 출감하기 일주일 전 교도소로 면회가 그를 만났던 남편하고 짜 맞춘 시나리오인지도 모릅니다.

다들 놀라시는군요.

garden after dark. It made my hair stand on end.

Worst of all was what happened to the fields.

It was rice-planting season, and everyone spent days on end irrigating the fields in preparation, flooding them with our well water. But then, when we actually went out to start the planting, there was no water left. It had all just—disappeared. Not only that, there were no traces of where it had been, no eel holes in the dirt banks, nothing, like some sort of ghostly trick. It had all been there, lapping at the edges; how could so much water disappear overnight? Where on earth could it have all gone?

At first everyone just scratched their heads and carried on planting, trying to refill the irrigation ditches with water from the creek. Before long, though, we realized that this was no different from pouring water into a jug with no bottom. The groundwater had been tapped so much that the surface kept drying up. Even when it rained, the water only sat for a day or two. It was only then that people started asking some real questions about all the groundwater the golf course was pumping up; that's when they started to understand what a truly huge amount of water must be necessary to keep those grassy greens from burning up

예, 놀라실 줄 충분히 알았습니다.

그런저런 시나리오에 대해 재판 과정에서 나조차 가타부타 말이 없었으니, 결과적으로는 당연히 그걸 사실이라 인정한 셈이 됐으니까요. 우리 변호사님은 내 침묵을 정말 마음 아파 하셨습니다. 아실는지 모르지만, 변호사님은 내 옛 친구의 남편이자, 은행에서 청원경찰을 하며 고시공부를 하던 분이신데요. 골프장을 고소하면 돈이 나온다, 상대편을 고발하면 합의금을 받을 수 있다, 그렇게 꼬시고 부추기는 다른 변호사님들하곤 다릅니다. 돈도 나오지 않는 이 재판을 위해 공주까지 벌써 두 번이나 손수 다녀온 분이시라구요.

이제 재판장님은 진실을 보고 들으실 겁니다.

나라고 번민이 없었던 게 아닙니다. 수백 번, 나 하나 뒤집어쓰면 그만이다, 생각했습니다. 변호사님의 설득이 없었다면 그랬을 거예요. 까짓 거, 얼마간 고생하다가 남편이 취하하면 끝나니까요. 몇 사람은 내가 간통한 여자라는 걸 기억하겠지만 모든 것이 깨어져 나간 판에 그것이 무섭겠습니까. 주홍글씨를 달고 다니라 할 것도 아니고요, 달고 다닌들 또 무슨 상관있나요. 내가 마음을 바꾼 건 나 살자고 바꾼 게 아닙니다. 어차피 우

under the beating summer sun. That awful golf course was pumping up every last drop of water they needed from our little village. It was true that they had been digging for water all along their ridge: it's just that they failed to find any. Lamentably, the only place rich with groundwater in that whole area turned out to be our little village.

They say that in one month, the golf course requires over seven hundred tons of water.

To make matters even worse, the golf course had started construction on a condominium. To train their employees on site, they had said. So when that was completed, their water needs would only increase. Basically, every month, a large lake was being sucked up into that golf course up there. And on top of that, the chemicals they used to maintain all that grass were so strong that any creek water that passed through the course was completely unusable. The rice stalks all went yellow long before harvest season, forcing the farmers to give up their crops entirely. They got together and went up to the golf course to protest, to demand compensation, but the people in charge were the picture of calm and relaxation.

They had already provided compensation, they

린 다 죽었고 다 깨어졌는걸요. 그렇지만 정말, 이대로 우리, 다 죽어도 좋은 걸까요.

변호사님, 녹음기를 틀어주세요.

부탁인데요, 재판장님, 길지 않습니다.

부디 막지 말아주세요. 녹음 내용엔 내가 마지막으로 반드시 해야 할 말들이 소상히 들어 있습니다. 파라다이스 여관 203호실에서 그날 무슨 일이 있었나, 그 진실에 대한 거예요. 내가 마음을 엊그제야 바꿨기 때문에 판결 직전인 오늘밖에 기회가 없었습니다. 그 점은 깊이 사죄드립니다. 변호사님이 증거품으로 제출하신다는 걸 마다하고, 굳이 내 마지막 진술 시간을 택해 공개하자는 것도 나의 뜻이었습니다. 지금은 필요한 대목만 틀겠습니다. 파라다이스 여관 203호실의 그날 그 시간으로 돌아가 보자는 겁니다.

예, 재판장님 허락해주셔서 고맙습니다.

(문 여닫히는 소리)

남자: 왜 그러고 서 있어. 웃옷이라도 벗지 않고…… 정말로 목간을 하고 싶었어…… 숙이 엄마가 오리라곤 전연 생각하지도 못했네. 제기랄, 이렇게 빨리 닥치다

explained, and the villagers themselves had signed away their consent, so, legally, the golf course was simply not at all liable; they had all the right papers.

And, indeed, among the papers the villagers were shown that day was the proof of their agreement, notarized and stamped with an official seal, that no one would protest the golf course's unrestricted use of the village groundwater, in perpetuity. Forever. What the villagers received in exchange, they had already been given: the fifty million *won*, long since split evenly between households, coming to thirteen million *won* per home.

People sought out my husband, then, along with the few representatives he had chosen that day, and hollered and screamed some more. But the results were the same. After all, they were the ones who had given my husband and the reps their power of attorney.

At one point, Foreman Suh's younger brother had grabbed the general manager by his collar, yelling, You said the golf course would only be taking a part of the water it needed from our village! In response, the general manager had smiled, and said:

Ah, well, we would have, you know, if we had found water on the course as well.

니…… 정말 놀라운 부부야, 부부가 짜고 한단 말은 못 들었거든.

여자: 무, 무슨 말인지 모르겠어요.

남자: 모르겠다니, 설명도 안 해주고 보냈다는 거야 뭐야. (이때 텔레비전 소리가 갑자기 들리기 시작, 대화가 들렸다 안 들렸다 한다) 진짜…… 머리 한번…… 끝내주는 작자야.

여자: 제발…… 내일까지만이라도 동네에 오지 말고…… 그 말을 하려고…… 원한다면…… 어떻게 해도 좋아요.

남자: 아이구, 손발…… 맞네그려…… 숙이 엄마, 너…… 이미현…… 맘 없어. 옛날…… 좋아했던 건 맞아…… 자원입대…… 니 학교에 찾아간 적…… 미칠 것 같아서…… 한번 부딪쳐나 보자고…… 너를 보자마자…… 기가 팍 죽더라고…… 음악실 뒤…… 송골송골 니 콧등에…… 죽을 때까지 정수리 안 갈 거야, 하던 네 말…… 그걸로 땡이야…… 공군에서…… 닦고 조이고…… 잊혀지더라구…… 너 때문에 홀아비로 지내는 거 아니니…… 오해…… 우는 거야?

여자: (우는 듯)

Enraged, Foreman Suh's younger brother took a swing at the man. Within the hour, a police car arrived from town to take him away on assault charges.

That same night, my husband and Foreman Suh came to blows for the first time. My husband ended up with a split lip and Foreman Suh got a bloody nose. My husband got a call from the golf course after that and went out, without a word to anyone, not even to me. All he said when he came back around lunchtime was: I reported the bastard.

As it turns out, the folks at the golf course had been kind enough to drive my husband all the way to the police station in town so that he could press charges against Foreman Suh. So it was Foreman Suh's turn this time to get hauled in, all before his younger brother had even been released. And then the day after that, we found out that Foreman Suh was pressing counter-charges, and so my husband was hauled in as well. They each spent a while declaring themselves to be the victim, but in the end they both withdrew the charges. This first incident was really the turning point where everyone started losing track of the actual essence of the problem at hand. After this, the fight we should have been tak-

남자: 젠장맞을, 왜…… 시간을 끈다는 거야, 준비했으면 빨리…… 닥치지 않고.

여자: (울먹이는 소리) 누가 닥친다는 거예요?

남자: 몰라서 물어? 이거…… 나도 뭐…… 좋아 그래라 한 건…… 씨발 것…… 이심에선 무조건 지게 돼 있다는 거야…… 우리 변호사 새끼…… 승소할 수…… 내 돈…… 후려 먹고…… 숙이 애비가 날 찾아온 것도…… 골프장에서……재판비용은……

여자: (놀란 듯) 그 사람이 면회를……

남자: 왜 몰랐어? (텔레비전 소리 뚝 그친다) 면회를 안 왔으면 숙이 엄마 덮치기로 한 거, 어떻게 짜 맞출 수 있었겠어. 그래도 그렇지. 이렇게 빨리, 더구나 숙이 엄마 너까지, 이렇게 자발적으로 동원돼 올 줄 정말 몰랐다. 니네 부부, 정말 독하다. 난 그저 적당할 때 너를 덮치는 시늉을 하다가 말야, 사람들한테 들켜서 큰 망신이나 떨라는 것으로 알아들었는데 말야. 하기야 뭐 골프장 놈들 머리에서 나왔겠지만. (문 쾅쾅 두들기는 소리) 인제 왔네. 파출소가 멀었던가 보지. (계속 문 두들기는 소리) 아까 교도소 앞에서 니 신랑 얼핏 본 것 같았는데, 선글라스를 끼고 있데. (문 밖에서 뭐라고 외치는 소리) 간첩놀이

ing to the golf course became fights between neighbors, between various factions in the village railing against one another. I didn't find this out until later, but even the police detective who advised Foreman Suh to press counter-charges, even this kind, helpful gentleman was actually known around the neighborhood as being in the pocket of the golf course. Which means, you see, that they were planning it all along. That even as they were pressuring my husband to press charges against Foreman Suh, they were counting on this counter-charge scenario.

Those were the fundamental principles at play.

It's a classic tactic, really. If the first tactic, as I said before, involves spreading some cash around to mess with people's minds, then the second tactic, too, is every bit as unimaginative and heavy-handed.

So what is this tactic, this method the rich and powerful have been using for the last thirty, forty years, this classic, conventional, almost traditional method that's still every bit as effective as it ever was? It's turning your opponents against one another. Divide and conquer.

Make this one suspect that one, make him dislike

를 하는 걸로 생각하나 보지.

(문 열리는 소란한 소리)

이게 그날의 진실입니다, 재판장님.

그가 텔레비전을 켜는 바람에 중간의 녹음 상태가 좋진 않지만요. 다시 들으시면 다 해석할 수 있으리라 봅니다. 녹음기는 침대 밑에 있었습니다. 그는 샤워를 끝내고 나와 웃통을 벗은 채 침대에 비스듬히 걸터앉아 있었구요, 나는 의자에 엉덩이를 붙인 듯 만 듯 팔걸이만 죽어라 붙잡고 있었지요. 파라다이스 여관, 공주교도소 부근, 203호실, 밖에 쨍한 여름햇볕 불타는 열한 시쯤의 풍경입니다. 여고 일 학년 때, 학교로 날 찾아왔던 얘기를 그가 먼저 했습니다. 그가 부부끼리 짰다 어쨌다 그런 말 했지만, 그때까지도 나는 전혀 그의 말을 알아들을 수 없었습니다. 음악실 뒤편, 커다란 버드나무 아래, 불과 삼사 분쯤이나 함께 어색하게 서 있었을까요. 행여 누가 남자와 서 있는 걸 볼까 봐 조마조마하면서, 그가 얼만큼 절박한 그리움으로 왔는지는 헤아릴 수 없고, 송골송골, 니 콧등에 땀방울 맺힌 골낸 모습, 그때 참 이뻤어, 라고 그가 말할 때, 참을 수 없이 눈물

him, hate him, revile him. Make people fight amongst one another and while they're so busy hating one another they completely forget what started it all in the first place. I may not have much schooling, but isn't this practically historical? Isn't this what they say England did to Africa, what America did to the Indians? Give this tribe a gun and have them kill that tribe, then go to that tribe, put a gun in their hand, and goad them into seeking their revenge. Keep on like that and, before long, it's a clean sweep. Like blowing your nose without using your hands.

That's how things stand right now in our neighborhood.

When he was elected last year, Foreman Suh brought a suit against the golf course in his capacity as the official village representative. His case was that the previous Village Foreman—that is, my husband—and his representatives had assumed power of attorney for the villagers and signed in their name when the villagers didn't actually have a full understanding of what was going on, and that this, in turn, rendered null and void any contract granting the golf course permanent unrestricted access to the groundwater. He insisted that there needed

이 쏟아졌습니다. 버드나무 가지는 바람에 흔들리고, 즐거운 곳에서는 날 오라 하여도…… 음악실에선 합창 연습이 한창이었습니다. 세상의 무게에 짓눌려서 자원입대로 세상에서 도망치기 직전의 그에게, 열여덟의, 순정에게, 나는 말했습니다. 다시 학교로 찾아오면 죽을 때까지 정수리에 돌아가지 않을 거야, 라구요. 내가 운 것은 그때가 그리워서 운 게 아닙니다. 그때의 우리는 지금보다 너무도 소중한 걸 많이 가졌구나, 하고 생각했구요, 과연 내가 이 여관을 다시 나갔을 때 정수리로 돌아갈 수 있을까, 하고 생각했지요. 눈물이 더욱 복받쳤습니다.

예예. 궁금한 게 있으신 거 압니다.

도대체 이게 뭐냐, 하고 물으시는 여러분의 눈빛, 이해합니다.

서 이장님은 골프장을 상대로 한 재판이 전혀 승산 없다는 걸 알고 있었습니다. 이장 선거 때까지라도 시간을 끌려고 항소를 했지만요, 항소할 때 이미 담당 변호사도 희망 없으니 손을 들자고 했다 들었습니다. 서 이장님은, 미쳐서, 논밭을 저당 잡히고 재판비용을 끌어다 썼습니다. 정말 미쳤던 거지요. 남편에 대한 증오

to be a new agreement, that for this kind of access to the groundwater, the golf course needed to provide at least a billion *won* in compensation, not to mention additional reparations for the losses resulting from several years of failed harvests.

Foreman Suh lost in the general court. As I said before, the villagers had only ever used the groundwater independently, as part of the use of their own private property, and the court found that this meant the village did not own communal rights to the resource. On top of that, there was also some question as to whether the Foreman was even an appropriate legal representative for the village, and all charges were summarily dismissed, And so Foreman Suh had to cover the legal fees for both sides.

The case is now being tried in a higher court, as a matter of course.

If the higher court overturns the ruling, it will, of course, be embarrassing for the golf course, but the real hardships will come to my husband and the individuals who helped him. You see, they will be deemed as having forged consent. I hear that the golf course is planning on suing them to cover their reparations, too, if it comes to it. They might

때문에 죽을 구멍으로, 전후좌우 가릴 것 없이, 냅다, 불붙은 쥐꼴이 되어 들어가 박혔으니 되돌아올 길이 안 보일밖에요. 그는 감옥에 들어앉아서 두세 달을 보낸 다음에야 자신이 죽을 구멍에 박혀 있다는 걸 깨달았던 겁니다. 이심에서의 판결도 보나마나 패소할 게 뻔하고요, 그럼 저쪽 재판비용까지 모조리 물어야 하고, 자기 편들던 아군들도 모두 등을 돌리겠지요. 그가 남편을 사기와 공문서 위조로 고소해 놓은 것도 골프장과 지하수 사용 무효소송과 맞물려 있으니, 패소할 게 정한 이치입니다. 무고죄로 몰릴 게 뻔하구요. 전답은 고사하고 얼마나 긴 옥살이를 또 해야 할는지 모를 판입니다.

미쳐 있기론 남편도 마찬가지였습니다.

서 이장이 감옥에 있을 때 남편이 골몰한 건 이장 자리입니다. 이장 선거는 서 이장이 출감한 뒤 불과 한 달 안에 치러지도록 되어 있었지요. 서 이장이 감옥에서 나오기 전에 마을 사람들의 인심을 얻어야 할 텐데, 밤낮없이, 이 돈 저 돈 끌어다가 마을 사람들 읍내로 데려가 술 사 먹이고 고기 사 먹이고 했지만, 효과는 없었습니다. 효과는커녕, 남편이 돈을 쓰면 쓸수록, 지하수 사용동의서를 써 주면서 골프장으로부터 한밑천 챙겼다

even be charged with fraud. So, basically, Foreman Suh's case against the golf course to declare the original groundwater contract invalid is actually driving my husband and his supporters to the edge of an impossible cliff. But, at the same time, win or lose, Foreman Suh still has to pay those legal fees, which means he'll still have to sell what little land he has. It's becoming a question of killing or dying for both sides.

This whole situation led to the incident where Foreman Suh beat my husband with the handle of a pickax, breaking his ribs and, thus, landing him in prison. All the while the golf course has taken a step back, quietly sitting it all out. After all, even if they lose the case, they have someone to sue for the damages. It would be a struggle to hang on to what little we have even if we all worked together. Instead we've all been swept up in this proxy war, just like the golf course intended. Eventually we're all going to end up dead. It's all part of a fundamental principle: the golf course has to teach us the kind of lesson we won't ever forget. This way no one will ever try to go up against them ever again. It's simple enough, women and children all understand it. I just don't know why no one else

는 소문만 확인해주는 꼴이 되었습니다. 감옥에 가 있는 서 이장에게 동정심이 몰리는 것도 필연일밖에요. 지난번 선거에선 단 한 표로 졌지만, 다가오는 선거에서 다시 이장이 되기는커녕 망신살만 뻗칠 거라는 걸 남편은 눈치챘습니다. 망신이 망신으로만 끝나면야 무슨 상관이겠습니까마는, 만약 돌아오는 이장 선거에 참패했을 때, 무엇보다 골프장 측이 헌신짝처럼 버린다고 생각하니 남편은 참을 수가 없었던 것입니다. 치욕도 치욕이려니와, 그 역시 죽을 지경이거든요. 나는 골프장과 남편 사이 어떤 야합과 묵계가 있는지 모릅니다. 지하수 사용동의서를 넘겨주며 남편이 어떤 대가를 받았는지도 알 수 없습니다. 그렇지만 지금의 남편 입장에서 다음 이장 자리는 절체절명 차지해야만 한다는 걸 알고 있습니다. 여러 고소 고발 사건도 이장이 되느냐 마느냐에 따라 판세가 달라질 거니까요. 그런데 희망은 점점 희박해졌습니다. 미칠밖에요.

재판장님, 나는 묻고 싶습니다.

남편이 공주교도소로 면회 간 일, 이러고저러고, 나를 겁탈하라고 했는지, 겁탈하는 시늉을 하라고 했는지는 분명하지 않지만요, 암튼 이장 선거를 앞두고, 사람들

seems to.

I'm sorry, I didn't mean to go on for so long.

My lawyer is giving me a look. I think he's saying it's time for me to start wrapping up. Or maybe he's just worried that I'll change my mind, that I won't go through with it. Your Honor, ladies and gentlemen in the gallery—though, of course, the gallery is mostly made up of our village elders—I know which story you've been waiting to hear. So let us, now, go to Paradise.

That was the name of the place near the Gongju Correctional Institute: the Paradise Motel. How did the opposing counsel phrase it earlier: stick to yes or no? Is it true that I entered the Paradise Motel with Foreman Suh?

Yes, it's true.

I entered the Paradise Motel.

Even after most of the crowd that was waiting for the other released prisoners had dispersed, Foreman Suh and I just stood awkwardly under the beating sun without saying a word, all the things we wanted to say caught in our throats. It was such a swelteringly hot day. The pavement in front of the prison gates felt as though it was boiling in the sun's harsh rays. I was sweating, and he was

인심을 결정적으로 잃게 하라는, 그러면 모든 고소를 취하하고, 그동안의 재판비용도 이쪽에서 맡겠다는, 더러운, 미친 야합이 과연, 남편의 머리에서 나왔을까요. 이 녹음테이프 더 정밀하게 들어보면요, 모든 재판비용, 골프장에서 대주기로 했다는 말이 나옵니다.

누군 또 물으시겠지요?

그까짓 이장, 포기한다면 되지, 뭐 그런 말도 안 되는 각본이 필요하겠느냐구요. 모르시는 말씀입니다. 서 이장은 이장 선거에 자의적으로는 불출마할 수 없게 돼 있습니다. 재판비용이나 그동안의 싸움질하는 데 든 돈, 서 이장 호주머니에서만 나온 게 아니에요. 그를 편들던, 여기도 와 계신, 여러 사람들도 돈의 일부를 댔습니다. 그것은 마을 사람 누구나 아는 사실이에요. 그 사람들 앞에, 옥살이 끝내고 나온 서 이장님이, 나 이장 그만할래, 해봐요. 서 이장님 맞아죽기 십상입니다. 그런 사정이야 뭐 남편 쪽도 마찬가지지만요.

사정은 또 있습니다.

완공을 앞두고 있는 골프장 내의 콘도미니엄.

말이야 직원연수를 위한 거라곤 하지만요, 우리 변호사님이 확인한 바로는 골프장 회원들을 상대로 이미 분

sweating. The few months of his term had left Foreman Suh even thinner than before, and his sweaty forehead looked dark and blotchy, his eyes sunk deep into his skull.

He's going to ask me why I came all the way here to Gongju, I thought, at first. And as the minutes passed I began to worry more about what my answer would be.

Of course, I knew the answer, inside.

You see, more than anything, I thought I needed to save my husband, and that I needed to save Foreman Suh, too. To save them both at once would be difficult, as difficult as they say it is for a rich man to go to heaven. But when my husband stepped out of our own gates with that sharpened scythe blade in his hand and murder in his eyes, I heard myself scream after him. No! I screamed. I couldn't just leave things alone. I couldn't just leave it to fate. I had to stop it. Whatever I had to do to stop it, if there was a way, even if it meant taking the blow of my husband's blade myself, or the bullets from the hunting rifle they said Foreman Suh's younger brother had bought—whatever it was, I was determined to do it.

But what could I say to my old friend there,

양신청을 받고 있다고 합니다. 골프장 측이 확보하고 있는 마을 사람들의 지하수 사용동의서엔 콘도미니엄 얘기가 없습니다. 그 동의서가 효력이 있더라도, 그건 어디까지나 골프장에서 사용하는 걸 동의한 거지 콘도미니엄에서 사용하는 걸 동의한 게 아니라는 것입니다. 골프장 측의 고민이 여기 있습니다. 골프장 측도 발등에 불이 떨어진 셈이죠.

서 이장은 죽어야 합니다.

골프장 입장에선 확실히 그렇지요.

이번 이장 선거는 물론이고 다음번에도 또 다음번에도, 영원히, 서경훈 씨가 이장이 되면 안 됩니다. 제일 좋은 건 아예 마을에서 살지 못하고 떠나는 거겠지요. 이 간통사건은 거기서부터 생겨났다고 나는 믿습니다. 정치판이든 장사판이든, 까놓고 말해, 우리 모두가 다 익숙한, 삼십 년 사십 년 전부터 지금까지, 여전히, 끈질기게, 그 생명력 자랑하는, 개뿔이나 상생은 무슨, 개떡이나 새천년은 무슨, 개코나 정보화 세계화는 무슨, 모두들 알고 있지요, 우리, 세상 눈부시게 변한다고 말들하지만, 이 수법 말예요. 면내의처럼 몸에 착 붙어서 이젠 진짜 우리 것이 돼 가고 있는, 이 더러운.

standing right in front of me? Should I have told him, My husband wants to kill you, he's carrying a scythe? Or maybe, Go ahead and kill me instead. Or, if you'd rather not kill me, then please just don't go back to the village today—come with me instead, someway far away, you always liked me, didn't you? Is that what I should have said?

But it wasn't me who broke that long, heavy silence. It was him. Wiping his hand across the sweat streaming down his neck, he said:

I need to wash. To shower.

I have no idea what the bathing facilities are like in prison. What I can say, though, is that when he said those words, he really looked as if he hadn't taken a single shower during his whole time in prison. But who knows? After being up all night, skipping breakfast, and standing for more than an hour under that summer sun, I might not have looked much better to him. We walked up the motel steps together—they were covered in red carpet; our steps didn't make a single sound. That's when my legs started to shake.

While I stood in the door to the motel room, hanging on to the doorframe, he stripped down with his back to me and went straight into the

이제 마무리를 할 시간이군요.

더러운 건 세상이 아니라 간통입니다. 그래요. 여러분은 한 더러운 여자를 보고 계십니다. 돌로 쳐야 할. 끝날 때가 오니까 저절로 그날 새벽의 일이 생각나는군요. 녹음기는 지난봄 큰애의 영어공부를 위해 사 준 겁니다. 문을 열고 나오려다가 돌아서 잠든 애들을 봤습니다. 큰애는 육 학년으로 곧 중학교에 가게 될 거고 작은 애는 삼 학년입니다. 계집애인 큰애의 소망은 비행기 여승무원이 되는 것입니다. 난 엄마 아빠처럼 이런 촌구석에서 안 살 거야. 큰애가 하던 말이 지금도 귓가에 쟁쟁합니다. 비행기를 타고 오대양 육대주 훨훨 날아다닐 우리 딸을 생각하니 눈물이 나는군요.

나는 녹음기를 핸드백에 집어넣었습니다.

충동적이었지만 강렬한 상상이 나를 후려쳤어요. 남편이 예전의 내 남편이 아니라는 것, 미쳤다는 것, 그거 알지만요, 나란히 누워 잠든 애들을 내려다보는 순간, 그를 버릴 수 없다, 그를 도울 수 있으면 도와야 한다, 그런 생각이 나를 후려치는 것이었습니다. 간통은…… 예정되어 있었습니다. 그들의 잔인하고 더러운 야합과 관계없이, 한편에선, 나와 나 사이에, 더욱 더러운, 끔찍

bathroom. For all the world it was like he was really just there for the shower.

Did I soap up his back for him?

Why not? Sure. Just like a scene in one of those fancy movies. They're saying that he unbuttoned my shirt with his wet hands in that bathroom, too. What a picture. Who can say who actually came up with this stuff? Maybe Foreman Suh worked up the scenario from movies he's seen, or maybe my husband fed it to him the week before, when he went to the prison to meet with him.

I see that surprises you all.

Yes, I knew very well that it would surprise you.

These scenarios have been coming up all through this trial and I've stayed silent. It makes sense that my silence may have seemed like an admission of guilt. I should tell you, no one felt my silence more keenly than my own lawyer. I don't know if you know this, but my lawyer is the husband of one of my oldest friends. And on top of that he worked as a security guard at my bank while he was studying to take the bar. He's different from all those other lawyers who kept badgering me to sue the golf course, to press countercharges against everyone in my own case, to get

한 야합이 만들어지고 있었던 거지요. 필요하다면, 작부처럼, 앞가슴이라도 드러내고 그를 유혹할 수 있다고 생각했습니다. 마침내 그들처럼, 나도 미쳐가고 있었지요. 한번 삐끗, 허당을 밟고 나면 모든 것이 아득해져서 제 구멍밖에 못 보는 것이 사람입니다. 그가 욕실로 들어갔을 때 나는 녹음기를 켜서 침대 밑에 밀어 넣었습니다. 분명한 시나리오가 있었던 건 아니었지만요, 암튼 이런 기회가 다시 올지 모르므로, 그와 간통한, 혹은 간통을 안 하더라도 여관에 들어와 있는 그 현장 증거를 확보해 두자고 본능적으로 느꼈던 것이지요. 아이들 아빠가 더 죽을 구멍으로 몰리면 써먹게 될지도 모르구요. 이장 선거를 앞두고 터뜨릴 수도 있구요. 또 협박할 수도 있습니다.

여관 문을 열자 남편이 순경과 함께 서 있데요.

남편은 다짜고짜 내 따귀를 호되게 갈겼습니다. 니 예펜네, 본래부터 날 좋아했었어. 이죽이죽, 서 이장이 말했고요, 남편이 달려들었으나 젊은 순경이 앞을 가로막았습니다. 교도소 앞에서 나와 마주 서 있을 때 나를 미행해 온 남편의 모습을 얼핏 보고 서 이장은 옳거니, 지금 여관으로 가라는 뜻이구나, 했던 것입니다. 어느 기

my own reparations. No, my lawyer is the kind of gentleman who's trekked all the way to Gongju twice already, and all for a case worth no money at all.

And now, Your Honor, you will see and hear the truth.

This wasn't an easy decision for me, either. Hundreds of times, I thought to myself that I could just take the fall, bring this business to a close. I probably would have, if my lawyer hadn't convinced me otherwise. After all, it wouldn't be so bad. Things would be rough for a little while. But then my husband would withdraw his complaint and it would all be over. Sure, a few people in the world would remember me as a cheater, but who would be afraid of something like that when everything else was falling apart? It's not as if I'd have to wear a scarlet letter. And really, even if I did, would that be so bad? I didn't change my mind about speaking up for my own benefit. I figure we're all already dead and everything's all over already. But then, is that acceptable? To just stand by and let it all end like this?

Play the tape, please.

Please, Your Honor. It's not very long.

회에 겁탈하려는 척해서 망신만 떨라는 것으로 생각했던 서 이장은 그 순간, 처음으로, 제대로 쓰인 간통 시나리오에 의해 자신이 움직이게 돼 있었다는 사실을 깨달았던 셈입니다. 녹음테이프엔 그때의 상황이 더 담겨 있습니다. 엊그제야 변호사님께 사실을 사실대로 말씀드렸는데, 용하게도 우리 변호사님, 공주까지 손수 내려가 그 녹음기를 찾아오셨네요.

결론은 이렇습니다.

구체적 행위가 있었든 없었든지 간에, 나는 한 남자의 아내로, 또 두 아이의 어머니로 이미 간통을 한 것과 다름없다는 사실입니다. 어디 간통뿐인가요. 그걸 녹음기에 담아두었다가, 내 이익을 지키는 데 필요하다면 서 이장님을, 어린 시절, 그 그리운, 향기 나는 우물 같은, 저기, 경훈 오빠를 수렁 속에 단번에 밀어 넣을 작정을 하고 있었던 여자예요. 예, 그래요. 이 아이러니를 뭐라고 해야 할는지요. 내가 법률적으로 간통하지 않았다는 걸 명백히 증거해주고 있는 이 녹음테이프, 이 녹음기야말로, 거꾸로 내가 도덕적으로, 그들만큼, 그들 이상 부서져서, 사악한, 간통자라는 걸 너무도 냉정하게 증명해주고 있다 그 말입니다.

Please don't stop this. The content of that recording covers everything I have left to say in minute detail. It's about what happened that day in Room 203 in the Paradise Motel, about the truth of what happened. The only reason it hasn't come up before now is that I only made up my mind to play it over the last few days—this is my last chance. My deepest apologies, Your Honor, for putting it off this long. My lawyer wanted to enter it as evidence right away; I'm the one who insisted that I wanted to wait until my final testimony to reveal it. I'll only play the relevant section of the tape right now. I'd like to take us all back to that hour, that day in Room 203 at the Paradise Motel.

Yes, Your Honor. Thank you for allowing this.

(Door opening/closing.)

Man: Why are you just standing there. Take off your top, at least... Man, I really needed that shower... You know, I never once imagined you'd come yourself. Jesus, you work fast... You're quite a set, the two of you. I didn't realize you were acting as a team.

Woman: I, I don't understand what you're talking

나는요, 간통한 여자입니다, 재판장님.

왜 이렇게…… 눈물이 나는지 모르겠네요.

돌 맞아 죽어도 싼 년답게…… 독하자, 했는데요. 이렇게, 모, 모두, 어머니인 나까지, 무너진, 불쌍한 우리들…… 때문에…… 눈물이…… 나서 몸 둘…… 바를 모르겠군요. 죄송합니다.

재판장님께 감사드립니다.

내 장광설을 참을성 있게 들어주셔서요. 그렇지만요, 웃기는 소리라고 하시겠지만요, 내가 결국…… 마음을 바꿔 녹음기 얘기를 한 것은 사실은…… 희망 때문이었어요. 변호사님이 그러시더라구요. 애들을 생각해보라구요. 희망을…… 남겨둬야 한다구요. 어머니는 때론…… 전사가 돼야 한다구요.

전사라니요, 재판장님.

나는 대학까지 못 간 게 마음속으로 오랜 한이었습니다.

글을 쓰고 싶었지요. 대학까지 갔더라면 유명한 시인이 됐을 거라고 상상한 적도 많아요. 읍내에 나가면 같이 시 쓰는 지역시인들이 장난으로 부릅니다. 이 시인, 이 시인 하고 말예요. 그들은 장난삼아 부르지만 난 그런 호칭으로 불릴 때마다 온몸이 부르르르 떨립니다.

about.

Man: Don't understand what I'm talking about? What, did they just send you here with no explanation? (A television is turned on; the conversation becomes difficult to hear clearly)...really...unbelievable...he's a mastermind.

Woman: Please... don't go to the village, just wait until tomorrow... just wanted to say... if you want... whatever you want with me.

Man: Oh for god's sake... sure... you... Lee Mihyeon... no thanks. It's true...long time ago I did...before I volunteered... went to your school...going crazy...just to see you, just once... the way you looked at me... felt so small...behind the music room...like dewdrops on your nose... You said, I will never come back to Jeongsu-ri, never... that was it... Air Force...stress...I managed to forget... You're not the reason I'm still single, so...don't flatter... are you crying?

Woman: (Crying)

아아, 시인…… 하고 나는 부르짖습니다.

그러나 이젠 시를 쓸 수 없습니다.

나의 깊고 향기로운 우물을 잃어버렸기 때문입니다.

삼 년 전, 지역 문학지에 당선한 나의 시를 심사한 교수이자 시인인 선생님은, 골프장 공사와 내 아이들의 희망을 빗대어 쓴 내 시를 두고, 서정적 감수성은 좋은데, 낡은, 거대담론적 시각 때문에 문제라고 평을 썼습니다. 거대담론은 문단에서도 폐기처분된 낡은 것이라구요. 골프장으로 줄을 잇는 덤프트럭들 소리에 우리 아이들이 자주 짜증을 낼 때였지요. 나는 거대담론이란 말이 무슨 뜻인지 몰라 몇 달을 헤맸습니다. 이제 그 시인 선생님을 만나면 뭔가, 말할 수 있을 것 같습니다. 사람이란 참 이상한 구석이 있어요. 어째서, 시를 쓸 수 없게 되자, 시인의 희망이 다 결딴나버리고 말자, 시에 대해서 말하고 싶은 것들이 이렇게 우아아, 아우성으로 생겨날까요.

다른 건 감히 바라지 않습니다.

나의 우물이 다시 차고, 검고 축축한 옷을 입은, 키가 너무 커서 꾸부정한 밤의 아저씨가, 한낮, 우물 밑에 누워 있다가, 저물녘, 사철나무 밑으로 성큼 나와 앉아, 물

Man: Damn it, why... they're taking so long. Just... over with, already.

Woman: (Still crying) Who... get what over with?

Man: You know exactly...about! I suppose...why I agreed...fucker...there's no way to win anymore... sorry excuse for a lawyer... sue... my money... all of it...why your husband came to see me... the golf course says... legal fees

Woman: (Shocked) He came to see...

Man: What, you didn't know? (The television is turned off.) Of course he came, how else would we have planned for me to attack you. But even so, this is happening so fast, and I just—I really had no idea you'd be here of your own accord like this. What a team, husband and wife. A couple of mercenaries. I thought I was just supposed to wait for an opportunity and pretend to attack you, then get myself caught in the act and humiliated. I mean, of course, this must all be coming from the brains of those golf course bastards. (Pounding on a door.) There they are. The police station must be far

레인지 풀무인지, 쓰윽쓰윽, 애들 장난하듯 돌려서, 멀고 가까운 데, 쓰윽쓰윽, 낮은 곳에서 높은 곳까지, 또 쓰윽쓰윽, 연기처럼, 먹물을 풀어 부드럽고 은근하게, 산의 원근도, 또 세상의 명암도, 쓰으윽, 가리는 걸 보고 싶습니다. 그러면 그 순정적 어둠 속에서, 사람들이 몰라서 그렇지, 단지 별만이 아니라 치자꽃, 그 이쁜 술잔 같은, 사철나무 잎새며, 망초꽃에 깃들인 애벌레며, 산초롱나무 잔가지가 뿜어내는 그 별빛, 모든 것들이, 제각각, 제몫몫 빛을 내고 있는 걸 보게 될 테니까요. 그 우물 곁에서 내 아이들과 함께 시 쓰는 상상을 하면 지금도 이렇게 진저리가 쳐집니다. 그래서요, 재판장님, 우리 변호사님 말처럼요, 지금 비록 내가 깨어지고 더러워졌으나, 아니 그러니까 더더욱, 난 갑옷을 입고 이제부터라도 천사가 아닌 전사가 되고자 합니다. 더러운 간통의 죄도 씻어야 하니까요.

꿈같이, 내 속에 우물 하나 품고서요.

『향기로운 우물 이야기』, 창비, 2000

away. (More pounding.) I thought I saw your husband earlier, out in front of the prison gate. He was wearing sunglasses. (Indecipherable yelling from outside the room.) He must be enjoying himself, playing the spy.

(Door opens, chaotic sounds.)

This is the truth of what happened that day, Your Honor.

I know the recording gets fuzzy here because he turned the television on, but if you listen again, you can make it all out. The recorder was under the bed. He had just finished his shower and stretched out on the bed with his shirt off; I was sitting on the chair, my bottom practically hovering over the seat, my hands gripping the chair arms. That was the scene in the Paradise Motel near Gongju Correctional Institute, Room 203, at around 11AM., with the sun beating down outside.

He brought up the time he came to see me during my first year at the girls' high school. He also said something about a husband and wife team, but at the time I truly had no understanding of what that meant. It was probably only three or four minutes, the time we spent standing awkwardly out back behind the school music room under that big weeping willow tree. I was so nervous someone would see me standing with a boy, I had no idea at all how much he must have missed me to come all that way. My nose was covered in sweat. Like dew drops, he said, and then: You were so pretty then. And that's when I started to cry. "Though the willow branches dance in the breeze/ Though you call to me from some lovely place..." That was the song they were practicing in the music room. And to that eighteen year old boy, a boy with the weight of the world on his shoulders, a boy about to join the military just to get away, to that innocence and sincerity, I said: If you ever come to my school again, I'll never come back to Jeongsu-ri, never. I cried in that motel room not because I missed those old times. I cried because it struck me: We had so many more precious things back then than we do now. And then I wondered, When I leave this motel, will I ever be able to go back to Jeongsu-ri? That just made me cry harder.

Yes, of course. I know you must have questions.

It's completely understandable, this searching look you're all giving me.

You see, Foreman Suh had come to understand

that all these suits against the golf course were ultimately fruitless. He kept up the fight to try and drag things out, at least until the next Foreman election, but I've been told that as early as the start of that first counter-suit, his lawyer had told him there was no hope of winning, that they should just give up. Foreman Suh, having lost his mind, had borrowed against his farmland to pay his legal fees. You'd have to lose your mind to do a thing like that. He loathed my husband so much that he had kept digging himself deeper into this mess, deeper and deeper like a rat on fire, until finally, he took a look around and there was no way out.

It was only after spending two, three months in prison that he realized the impossible position he was in. It was obvious what the higher court would rule, and that would just mean more legal fees for both sides that he would have to pay. It wouldn't be long before all his supporters turned their backs on him, too. The charges he'd brought against my husband for fraud and counterfeiting were all tied in with the original case about the groundwater contract with the golf course, so it was only logical that he would lose those as well. It was clear that he would be found guilty of libel, and, his farmland aside, who knew how much more time he would have to spend in prison?

In terms of going crazy, my husband was no different.

The whole time Foreman Suh was in prison, my husband was focusing on winning back his seat. The elections for Village Foreman were scheduled to take place less than one month after Foreman Suh was getting out of prison. My husband had to win back the people of the village before Foreman Suh's release, and he certainly tried, scrounging up money here and there to whisk people off into town, day and night, for expensive meals and drinks.

But it was no use. In fact, it had opposite effect: the more money my husband spent on the villagers, the more likely it seemed that the rumor—my husband had pocketed a tidy sum from the golf course for getting them that consent contract—was actually true. It was inevitable that people would start feeling sympathetic for Foreman Suh sitting up in his prison cell. My husband realized that even though he had only lost by one vote in the previous election, the coming one was shaping up to be an outright humiliating loss.

This potential humiliation was one thing, but he also knew that if he lost badly in the upcoming election, the golf course would toss him aside like a used slipper—and this, he could not abide. The indignity alone would have been bad enough, but this would have put him in an impossible fix of his own. I have no idea what kind of plots or tacit understandings are in place between my husband and that golf course. I have no idea what sort of compensation my husband received for handing over the groundwater contract. But I do know that in his current position, it was vital that my husband win the election or die trying. Because when it comes down to it, all these different court cases hinge on who the Village Foreman is. But his hope just kept on dwindling. The only option left was for him to lose his mind.

Your Honor, I would like to ask the following.

It may not be clear exactly what was discussed when my husband went to the Gongju Correctional Institute to meet with Foreman Suh. There is no way of knowing whether Foreman Suh was told to rape me, or pretend to rape me. But what is clear is that Foreman Suh was meant to shame himself before the upcoming election, to lose the trust of the people completely. It's clear he was told that if he did this, all lawsuits would be withdrawn. All the legal fees accrued to date would be paid. Can this filthy, crazy conspiracy have possibly come from the mind of my husband? If you listen more closely to this tape, Foreman Suh explains that all those legal fees, every last bit, was going to be paid by the golf course.

Someone or other is guaranteed to ask:

Why not just withdraw from the elections? Why all this crazy plots and dramatic schemes? But this someone would be mistaken. There was no way Foreman Suh could just stop running for the office. All those legal fees, all the money that had gone into this fight, it didn't all just come from Foreman Suh. Much of it came from his supporters, from many of the people sitting here today. Everyone in our village knows that. So just imagine Foreman Suh, fresh out of prison, standing up in front of these same people and announcing, You know, I just don't feel like being Foreman anymore. He'd probably be beaten to death. And, of course, all this goes for my husband, too.

There's something else to consider as well.

The golf course condominium that's nearing

completion.

They say, of course, that it's for on-site employee training, but, according to my lawyer, the golf course is already accepting applications from its members for various units. The groundwater usage contract the golf course currently holds has no mention of the water being used for any condominium. Even if the contract was deemed legal, it only covers use of the groundwater for the course itself; no one ever agreed to the condominium's usage. This is what the golf course is concerned about. The golf course, too, must move quickly.

Foreman Suh must die.

From the perspective of the golf course, nothing could be clearer.

Not just in this election but in the next, and in all the elections thereafter, forever, Mr. Suh Gyeong-hun must never be elected Foreman again. Indeed, the best-case scenario would be if he was no longer allowed to live in the village and had to leave the area altogether. I believe all this talk of rape started there. It's that same old tactic, whether in politics, or business, to put it plainly, that same thing we're all used to from the last thirty, forty years that's still being used today, that same persistent, undying thing. All this nonsense about cohabitation, about the new millennium, the information age, the global age, we all hear it, we all talk about it, we say the world has changed, shiny and new, but this thing remains. Sticking to us like a cotton slip, this filth. It's becoming a part of us now.

I suppose it really is time to wrap things up.

What's really filthy here isn't the world, it's adultery. You're right. You all are looking at one filthy woman, ladies and gentlemen. Should be stoned. Now that I'm almost done my thoughts are turning naturally back to that early morning. I first bought that tape recorder for my older child last spring, to use for learning English. As I was stepping out of our open front door, I looked back and saw my sleeping children. My oldest is in sixth grade, about to start middle school, and my youngest is in third grade. The older one, a daughter, wants to be a flight attendant someday.

I'm not gonna live in some tiny little village in the middle of nowhere like you and dad, she told me.

Thinking of her flying all over the world, over five seas and seven continents—it brings tears to my eyes.

I put the tape recorder in my purse.

It was just a passing impulse that made me take it, but immediately my imagination started working. I know my husband is no longer the man I married, that he's lost his mind, but in that instant when I looked down on our sleeping children, I knew that I couldn't just toss him aside, that I had to help him if I could. It was a realization that seared itself across my soul.

As for the adultery... well, that just came right on schedule. Knowing nothing about all their malicious, filthy conspiring, I was conspiring myself on this side of things. An even filthier, more unthinkable conspiracy between me and me.

If necessary, I told myself, I would lay bare my breasts like a bargirl: I would seduce him. Just like them, I was finally losing my mind, too. That's human nature: one misstep and everything else grows distant somehow. All you can see is what's right in front of you. When he went into the bathroom I turned the recorder on and pushed it under the bed. It's not as though I had a specific plan, but I did know that I might not get this kind of chance again, and I knew, instinctively, that I had to get some sort of evidence of our adultery. Or, if no adulterous act actually came to pass, then at least evidence of us both being in a motel together. I thought that if things kept getting worse for the father of my children, I might be able to use it to help him. Maybe circulate it before the next village elections. Maybe threaten Foreman Suh with it.

When the motel door opened my husband was standing there next to the police.

The first thing my husband did was slap me across the face. Hard. This woman of yours, you know, she always had a thing for me. That's what Foreman Suh said, grinning.

My husband tried to hit him, then, but a young policeman stopped him. Back in front of the prison gates, Foreman Suh had caught a glimpse of my husband, who'd followed me there, and thought, Ah, they must want me to go to the motel now. Having thought until that moment that he would just look for his chance, pretend to rape me, and humiliate himself, that this was the plan, it seems it was only in that moment in front of the prison that he realized that he was a player in an actual adultery scenario. There's more on the recording that explains the situation further. It was only a day or two ago that I finally told my lawyer the truth about everything. That's when he went all the way to Gongju to find the tape recorder and bring it back.

The conclusion is as follows.

Whether or not a specific act was committed, as a wife who has a husband, and as the mother of two children, there is no denying the fact that I have already committed adultery. Indeed, I've done a great deal more than that. I recorded this adultery, and, if necessary, to protect my own interests, I was planning on using it to ruin Foreman Suh sitting right there. I was going to ruin Gyeong-hun *Oppa*, the Gyeong-hun *Oppa* of my childhood, that boy I missed so much, that boy so like a fragrant well himself.

That's the kind of woman I am. Yes, that's right. What more to say about this ironic turn? This recording that clearly proves I did not commit adultery in the eyes of the law, this same recording stands as incontrovertible evidence that, morally, I am every bit as bad as—no, worse than—they are. It proves beyond the shadow of a doubt that I am an evil adulteress. Your Honor, I am a woman who has committed adultery. I am a woman who deserves to be stoned by everyone present.

I don't know why... I keep crying like this.

I told myself to be cold... like the kind of woman who deserves to be stoned to death. But thinking about how we've fallen, me, a mo, mother, and all of us, in this pitiable state... it just... brings tears to my eyes... I don't know what to... do with myself. I'm so sorry. I would like to thank you, Your Honor, for listening so patiently to this lengthy speech of mine.

But you know, you may say find this laughable, but the thing, in the end... the thing that made me change my mind, in the end, and tell the truth about the recording... it was hope. That's what my lawyer told me. That I had to think of the children. That I had to leave room for... hope. That sometimes a mother... has to be a warrior.

I'm no warrior, Your Honor.

It always bothered me that I never got the chance to go to university. I wanted to write, you see. I used to imagine all the time that if I'd just gone to college, I could have become a famous poet. When I go into town, a few of the local poets I write poetry with will tease me a bit sometimes, calling me Poet Lee, Poet Lee. They're only playing around, but whenever they address me that way, it still sends tingles up and down my whole body. Ahh, to be a poet!

But I won't be writing any more poetry now.

Because I've lost that deep, fragrant well of mine. Three years ago, when I won that poetry prize in the local literary magazine, a professor and poet who was one of the judges sent me a critique. The poem was inspired by the construction of the golf course and the hopes of my children. The professor explained that while there was a good lyrical sensibility at play in the piece, the outdated, macro-discursive perspective was problematic. This was right around when my children were often all about the noise from all the dump trucks constantly passing back and forth from the golf course. Not having any idea what 'macro-discursive' might have meant, I fretted over this for several months. Now, though, if I ever run into this professor poet, I think I might have something to say. We human beings are really quite strange, in a way. Now that I can't write poetry anymore, now that I've completely surrendered the dream of becoming a poet, it's as if I have more than ever I want to say about poetry, as if it's all just clamoring to get out.

I don't dare to hope for anything different.

I want to see my well fill up again, to see that

gentleman, the night, in his black, damp clothes, so tall he's bent slightly at the waist, at high noon, lying still at the bottom of the well, and then, at nightfall, coming out to sit under the spindle tree with his water wheel, or bellows, spinning like some children's game, swish swish, near and far, swish swish, high and low, swish swish, like smoke, like bleeding ink in water, soft and subtle, covering it all up, the lines of the mountains, swish swish, the light of the world. Then, finally, in that pure darkness, we'll be able to see it—not just from the stars but from the gardenia blossoms, those pretty ceramic cups, and the leaves of the spindle tree, and the grub between the flower petals, and smallest spiderwebbing branches of the lantern tree—we'll see the light coming off all of these things, each of these things, and more. When I imagine sitting by that well with my children, writing a poem together, it sends shivers up my spine even now, in this moment.

So, Your Honor, like my lawyer said, though I've fallen along the way, and dirtied myself—or rather, because of that—I plan to put on my armor and start, even if only now, on becoming a warrior instead of an angel. After all, I have this filthy sin of adultery I still need to wash away.

With a well of my own to cherish within me, like a dream.

Translated by Maya West

해설

Afterword

밤빛을 우려내는, 깊고 향그러운 우물

오태호 (문학평론가)

여기, 유년시절의 추억과 자본의 비정한 현실을 상기시키는 '우물'이 하나 있다. 농촌 공동체 사회에서 '순정한 어둠'의 빛을 내장한, 그 '깊고 향그러운 우물'을 내면에 품은 한 여인이 법정에 선다. 한 여자의 '법정 진술'로 이루어진 작품은 구어체적 표현이 제공하는 생동감 속에, 문제가 '간통'이 아니라 '골프장 건설'에 있었음을 드러낸다. 일종의 추리소설적 형식을 내장한—향기로운 우물 이야기—는 문단 경력 사십여 년의 적공이 빚어낸 작가의 서사적 장악력을 온전히 보여준다.

법정에서 최후 진술을 하는 여인의 입장을 중심으로 볼 때, 이 사건은 '간통'이 아니라 '골프장 건설'에 의해

The Light of Night and the Deep, Fragrant Well

Oh Tae-ho (literary critic)

What we have here in Park Bum-shin's newest story, "The Fragrant Well," is something that both calls to mind our most cherished memories of childhood and elicits the cold-hearted reality of capitalism. A woman takes the stand, a woman who has internalized the image of a "deep, fragrant well," and who claims that light that can be found in the "innocent darkness" of a small farming village and its intimate community. Told as the final testimony of a woman's court trial, the narrative employs colloquial registers to suspend our disbelief so as to bring us to the understanding that the heart of the trial is not, in fact, centered around

마을 공동체가 붕괴된 현실이 주요 핵심에 해당한다. 이렇게 보면 이 작품은 '향기로운 우물'을 품었던 정수리 마을이 골프장 건설로 인해 두 패로 나뉘어 자중지란으로 고소, 고발 사건이 진행되는 이야기를 다루고 있는 것으로 여겨진다. 하지만 그 표면적 이야기의 깊은 속내를 파고들어가 보면 원초적 고향을 환기하는 상징으로 '깊은 우물'의 향기와 '검은 밤빛'의 이미지가 자리한다. '깊은 우물'과 '검은 밤빛'은 이 작품의 구심적 기능을 담당하며, 화자의 유년시절과 현재를 마주 보게 함으로써 진실을 드러내는 열쇠어에 해당한다.

간통 사건으로 법정 진술대에 선 여인(화자 '나', 이름 미현)은 사건의 본질이 간통에 있지 않음을 강조한다. '예, 아니오'를 강요하는 이분법적 심문의 부당성을 지적하던 여인은 친정집 뒤란에 있던 우물을 떠올린다. 그 우물과 사철나무의 그늘에서 풍기는 '어둠의 먹물'은 유년시절을 낭만적으로 환기하게 만드는 원형적 상징이기 때문이다. 그 상징은 남편과 대척점에 서 있는 간통 사건의 또 다른 주인공인 서경훈 이장(경훈 오빠)에 의해 유년시절 이후 화자 내면에 스며든다. 서 이장이 유년시절의 '나'에게, 낮에는 깊은 우물 밑에 축축한 검은 옷

adultery, but rather the construction of a golf course in the area nearby. With a structure reminiscent of a mystery genre, "The Fragrant Well" is a product worthy of the author's thirty-year career, showcasing the impressive breadth of his narrative command.

Framed from the perspective of the woman giving her final testimony in court, Park's story presents the construction of a golf course rather than a supposed act of infidelity as at the root of the village's communal breakdown. Indeed, in this light, the actual focus of the story becomes the way in which the construction of a golf course leads to the divisions and infighting, indictments and lawsuits that plague the story's idyllic village setting of Jeongsu-ri, known for its "fragrant wells" and near mystical-quality water. If we look beyond even this, however, and investigate the possible underlying intentions of the piece as a whole, we are faced with images of a "deep well" and a "black light of night"—both reminders of an almost prehistoric home. This "deep well" and "black light of night" act as pivots on which the entire story turns, bringing the narrator's childhood face to face with her present in what is ultimately a revelation of

을 입고 숨어 있다가 해가 지면 나타나는 '밤'이, 사철나무 밑에서 검은 물레를 돌리며 연기를 피우듯 온 세상에 어둠을 피워놓는다고 이야기해 주었기 때문이다.

그때 화자는 '불순한 빛'이 아니라 '순결하고 순정한 어둠'에서 모든 존재자들이 뿜어내는 빛의 아름다운 현현을 상상한다. 거기에는 밤이면 우박처럼 머리 위로 쏟아져 내리던 별빛의 아름다움과 흰 꽃 위로 쏟아져 내리던 달빛의 숨막힘이 있다. 특히 달빛에 실린 치자꽃 향기가 화자의 온 실핏줄과 온몸의 모공(毛孔)을 모두 열어젖히는 '희열의 순간'을 제공한다. 하지만 그 밤빛과 희열의 체험은 골프장 가로등이 마을에 생기면서 사라진다. 그러므로 골프장 건설은 향기로운 우물의 기억을 소멸시킨 자본의 테러 행위에 해당한다.

하지만 자본의 고전적이고 상투적인 수법을 외면한 채 골프장 건설을 찬성하는 남편은 골프장 건설을 반대하는 서 이장의 교도소 출감을 앞둔 날 밤에 낫날을 날카롭게 갈아대면서 자신의 분노와 적개심을 드러낸다. 그 낫날의 '흰 광채' 앞에서, 화자는 하얀 치자꽃들의 목이 잘리는 '잔인한 낙화'를 상상한다. 육 년 전 '향기나는 우물'을 상상하며 고향에 왔을 때는 남편과 경훈오빠가

truth.

The accused adulterer on stand, the narrator Mi-hyeon, emphasizes that the essence of the case does not, in fact, have anything to do with adultery. Pointing out the inherent limitations of the dichotomous insistence of "yes" or "no" during her questioning, the woman recalls the well out back behind her old family home. She does this because that very well, along with the inky darkness that would spread from the shade of the spindle tree, are symbols that allow a romantic revisiting of her childhood years. These symbols have been intrinsic parts of her ever since her childhood due to the influence of the third party embroiled in this so-called adultery case, the character known to most of the villagers as Foreman Suh or, as the narrator occasionally remembers him, Gyeong-hun *Oppa*, the character set in diametric opposition to the narrator's husband. It was Foreman Suh who told her as a child the story of how the night hid at the bottom of a well, wearing "damp, black clothes," and crept out at dusk to sit under a spindle tree and spin its black water wheel, spooling darkness like smoke all over the world.

At this point, the narrator imagines the beautiful

죽이 잘 맞았지만, 이 년 전 골프장 건설로 인해 마을사람들의 의견이 양분되면서 서로 대립하게 된 것이 이 지경에 이른 것이다. 화자는 골프장 측이 파놓은 함정이 간통 사건이라면서, 간통이 아니라 골프장이 문제라고 재판장에게 하소연한다.

골프장 건설 이후 가든과 여관만 생겨나고, 남편은 서 이장을 폭행, 무고, 협박, 명예훼손으로 고소하고, 서 이장도 남편을 폭행, 무고, 공문서 위조, 사기 등으로 고소하면서, 남편파와 서 이장파 사이는 원수지간이 된다. 더구나 공동수도 공사 이후 골프장이 개장되면서 재래식 우물과 논물이 말라버리자, 화자는 더 이상 '검은 옷을 입은 밤'에 매료되지 못한다. 이제 밝은 가로등 아래에서 밤과 어둠을 무서워하게 된 것이다.

화자는 골프장 측의 입장에서 보면 서 이장이 죽어서 사라지거나 영원히 이장이 되면 안 되기 때문에 '간통 사건'을 작위적으로 조작한 것으로 판단한다. 그러나 그럼에도 불구하고 화자는 구체적 행위 여부와는 상관없이 자신이 이미 간통을 한 것과 다름없다고 진술한다. 자신의 이익(혹은 가족의 이익)을 지키기 위해 '향기나는 우물 같은' 경훈 오빠를 수렁 속에 단번에 밀어 넣을 작

incarnation of light given off by all things in a "pure, innocent" kind of darkness. In this light, the loveliness of the starlight pours down like hail, moonlight spills breathlessly over a sea of white flowers. Here, especially, is the moment of ecstasy brought on by the scent of gardenias in moonlight, a scent that opens every capillary and every pore in the narrator's body. Unfortunately, this thrilling nighttime light, this sort of sublime reveling, disappears under streetlights installed across the village by the golf course. In this way, at least, the construction of the golf course is nothing less than an act of terrorism that renders extinct all memory of those fragrant wells.

Meanwhile, the narrator's husband, in support of the golf course and willfully blind of these "classic" and "conventional" tactics of the golf course's capitalist powers, greets the release of the prisoner and his opponent Foreman Suh by staying up all night to sharpen the blade of his scythe, thereby revealing the depth of his own rage and enmity towards him. Before seeing the revealing glint of her husband's scythe, the narrator imagines a "cruel scattering" of white gardenias, slicing through a neck. Despite the fact that the narrator's husband had fast

정이었기 때문이다. 화자가 여관에 설치한 녹음기는 화자의 '간통 부재'와 '사악한 간통'을 동시에 증명해주는 '실재와 부재'의 동시적 알리바이가 된다. 실제적으로는 간통이 부재했지만, 상상적으로는 이미 간통을 수행한 것이나 다름없기 때문이다. 그러나 화자는 녹음기를 통해 골프장 측의 음모가 밝혀지면서 '깊고 향기로운 우물'에 대한 희망을 상기하고자 했음을 진술한다. '상실된 우물'에 대한 절망을 '우물의 채움'에 대한 희망으로 전환하기 위하여 화자는 골프장 측과의 싸움을 위한 '전사'가 되기로 작정한 것이다.

화자는 자신의 우물(=고향의 우물)이 다시 채워지고, '검고 축축한 옷을 입은 밤의 아저씨'가 사철나무 밑으로 나와 앉아 먹물을 풀어 은근하게 산의 원근과 세상의 명암을 가리는 걸 보고 싶어 한다. 그 '순정한 어둠' 속에서 모든 것들이 제각기 제 몫의 빛을 내고 있는 것을 볼 수 있기 때문이다. 화자는 '간통 사건'으로 법정에 서면서 자신이 깨어지고 더러워졌으나 이제 갑옷을 입고 천사가 아닌 전사가 되어, 실제로는 부재하는 '더러운 간통'의 죄를 정화하고자 한다. 그것은 '마을의 향기'와 '우물의 빛깔'을 되찾기 위해 '꿈'처럼 자신의 내면에

befriended Foreman Suh six years earlier when she first moved back to the village dreaming of fragrant wells, the construction of the golf course over the past two years has split all the villagers into two opposing camps with Suh and the narrator's husband as their heads. At the time of the trial, they remain at an insoluble impasse. The adultery case itself, according to the narrator, is simply a trap set by the golf course to resolve the characters' conflict in their favor. Again and again, she protests to the court that the issue here is not the adultery, but the golf course.

Once the construction of the golf course is complete and the area becomes overrun with restaurants and motels, the narrator's husband presses charges against Foreman Suh for assault, false accusations, threats, and libel, while at the same time Foreman Suh presses counter-charges against him for assault, false accusations, government document counterfeiting, and fraud. And as the golf course opens for business and the public water system is completed, decimating the village's wells and fields in the process, the narrator is no longer able to experience the enchantment of her village's particular night in its nighttime garments. Under the

'우물 하나'를 품으려는 다짐으로 이어진다.

「향기로운 우물 이야기」는 전통적 마을 공동체 사회를 지탱하던 '우물의 깊은 향기'가 골프장 건설로 소멸되는 자본주의적 현실을 비판한다. 골프장으로 대변되는 대자본의 논리는 마을 공동체의 인간적 유대 관계를 일거에 붕괴시킨다. 분열주의적 자본의 공작이 마을 주민들의 이기적 욕망 앞에 자중지란을 낳게 한 것이다. 그리고 마을의 양분화는 자신들의 생활 터전뿐만 아니라 공동체의 증거인 '향기로운 우물'의 멸실을 가져온다. 그러므로 화자는 전사가 되어 '향기나는 우물'을 지키기 위해 법정에서 간통 사건 이면에 감추어진 공동체적 진실의 진술을 감행하는 것이다. '깊은 우물'과 '검은 밤빛'의 낭만적 이미지를 간직한 어머니를 법정에서 대자본의 이윤 추구에 맞서는 전사로 키우는 시대가 자본주의 시대의 비정한 현실임을 비판하고 있는 작품이 바로 「향기로운 우물 이야기」인 것이다. 그 비판이 직설적인 이항대립적 거대 담론의 저항 논리로부터 비껴 설 수 있는 까닭은 작가가 밤빛을 우려내어 상징화한 '깊고 향기로운 우물' 이미지에 있을 것이다.

brightness of the new streetlights she has learned to fear the darkness and the night.

The narrator believes that the accusation of adultery that she faces is nothing but a fabrication created entirely by the minds of the golf course powers all in order to make Foreman Suh disappear for good or, at the very least, keep him from ever being reelected as Foreman. And yet, despite denying all charges of any sort of conventional infidelity, the narrator testifies that she has, in effect, still committed adultery. She bases her claim on the fact that she was willing to betray "Gyeong-hun *Oppa*," a person once so like a fragrant well himself, in the service of her own good, or, rather, her family's good. The tape recorder she took with her into the motel room comes to serve as proof that she did not commit the act while also proving her readiness to do so: in effect, it provides an alibi for her absence and presence simultaneously. While no literal act of adultery took place, in her mind it is no different than if it had. Still, the narrator testifies that, as the recording has revealed the nature of the golf course's conspiracy, she has been able to revive her hopes for her deep and fragrant well. In order to transform her despair over the lost well into a hope that could someday fill a well of her own, in this way the narrator has found the will to become a "warrior' in the battle against the golf course.

The narrator hopes her own well—the well of her personal home—will come to find itself filled again; she hopes to see once more that gentleman night in his black, damp clothes, coming out to sit under the spindle tree to spin his inky darkness over the mountain lines, the light of the world. In this idyllic sort of darkness, it becomes possible to see how every last thing in this world gives off a light of its own. Taking the stand to testify in this trial of adultery, the narrator acknowledges that she has been broken, and dirtied. At the same time, however, she seeks to don her armor to become a warrior rather than the redemptive, or even martyred angel, to cleanse herself of this sin, this filthy act of infidelity that never actually even took place. This leads to a concluding determination to once more cherish a well of her own, within herself—to recover, in other words, the fragrance of the village, the light of the well.

"The Fragrant Well" stands as a critique of a capitalist reality in which the deep scent of a well that once sustained a traditional way of life in a village community could be so easily annihilated by something like the construction of a golf course. This golf course, a stand-in for the logic of big capital, destroys the human bonds that hold the village community together in one fell swoop. The schism resulting from this capitalist sabotage soon has the villagers giving in to their selfish desires and fighting amongst themselves. This division, in its turn, causes the breakdown of not only their village life, but of the wells that served as proof of their community's strength. Indeed, it is in order to protect this "fragrant well" that the narrator ultimately embraces the role of a warrior in the court of law, undertaking a testimony of communal truth that lays bare the dark side of the adulterous incident in question. "The Fragrant Well" can then be understood as a story that criticizes the cold-hearted reality of this capitalist age, charting the way this same reality has forced an ordinary mother—one who still cherishes the romantic images of a 'deep well' and the "black light of night"—to transform herself into a warrior fighting against the blind pursuit of profit that characterizes big capital. As for what keeps this critique from falling under the category of a straightforward, binary, "macro-discursive" logic of resistance—we should look to that same symbol, steeped in the night's transformative light, the image of that "the deep and fragrant well."

비평의 목소리

Critical Acclaim

일상적인 자아를 발견한 이 작가의 삶이 감동을 주는 것은 풍랑을 이기고 불멸의 욕심을 버린 작가적 깨달음만이 아니라 평상심의 상태에서 삶의 깊이를 획득해가는 그의 평온한 관찰력 때문이다. 작가의 침묵이 이처럼 생산적인 결과로 나타난 것을 감동 없이 읽을 수 없다. 여기에는 과장 없는 진솔함이 잔잔하게 깔려 있다. 야성적인 그의 세계가 세련성을 획득하고 있음을 확인할 수 있다.

김치수

작가의 운명은 신비롭다. 창작의 절정에서 저 깊은 침

The reason we cannot help but be moved by the life of this author—who found himself in a particularly demanding kind of everyday life—isn't because he has overcome the roughest winds and waves to reach a writerly understanding that allowed him to cast aside the desire for immortality; no, we cannot help but feel moved because of his powers of peaceful observation, a power that has allowed him to acquire a true depth of life within his day-to-day heart and mind. When a writer's silence results in the manifestation of this kind of productivity, it is impossible to read the results without being touched. Here we have a bed of tranquil sincerity

묵 속으로 추락하는가 하면, 밑 모를 바닥에서 눈부시게 부활하기도 한다.『흰소가 끄는 수레』로 작단에 복귀한 이래, 박범신은 이순(耳順)을 바라보며 창작의 청춘을 구가한다. 최근 이 년간의 작업을 모은『향기로운 우물 이야기』에서 작가는 현재를 과거와 마주 세우고 농촌과 도시를 아우르며 정통 사실주의에서 마술적 리얼리즘에 이르는 다양한 기법을 실험하면서 날카로운 전환기를 맞이한 우리의 삶을 해부하고 있다.

최원식

초기의 단편들 속에서 작가는 도시문명과 자본주의의 음험한 욕망이 침투함으로써 피폐해지거나 타락해가는 농촌의 실상을 비판하고 그것에 분노하거나 좌절하는 시선을 드러낸 바 있다. 그런데 이번에 발표된『들길』 연작에서 돋보이는 작가의 시선은 농촌의 뼈저린 가난과 고통을 견디어내게 만드는 가족애와 삶의 본원적인 생명력에 머물러 있다. 아마도 리얼리즘에 뿌리를 내리는 그의 서사적 추동력을 만들어내는 근본은 그러한 가족애와 삶의 본원적인 생명력에 대한 믿음에서 비롯되었을 것이다.

free of exaggeration. Here we can see a writer's once wild world now grown refined.

Kim Chi-su

The destiny of a writer can be mysterious: he may plunge deep into a lengthy silence at the peak of his creative powers, only to rise from the bottom of these unknowable depths in a brilliant rebirth. Since returning to the literary scene with *The Cart Pulled By the White Cow*, Park Bum-shin has conquered the heights of a youthful, vibrant prose even as he approaches his sixtieth year of life. In his recent *The Fragrant Well*, a collection of his work from the last two years, Park sets the present against the past, the city together with the country, and experiments with a diverse array of techniques including both traditional realism and magical realism, all in the service of dissecting our lives in the face of such a sharp turning point in history.

Choi Won-sik

In his earlier works, Yi directed his critical eye at the ways in which the sinister appetites of urban civilization and capitalism have penetrated—and thereby impoverished and corrupted—rural reality,

작가는 『들길』 연작을 통하여 옛 고향의 "모든 것들이, 제각각, 제뭇뭇 빛을 내고 있는"(「향기로운 우물 이야기」) 풍경을 복원하고 싶어 하는데, 그것을 가능하게 하는 동인이 가족애와 삶의 본원적인 생명력에 대한 믿음일 것이다. 이제는 사라져가는 가족애와 본원적인 삶의 생명력을 다시 한번 퍼올릴 수 있는 '향기로운 우물'을 그는 꿈꾸고 있는 것이다.

이경호

revealing his own rage and frustration. In his more recent *The Field Path*, however, the author's gaze dwells instead on the love of family and a kind of original life force—the very things that render the pain and poverty of rural life bearable. Arguably, the very engine of Yi's narrative impulse, rooted in realism, is fueled by this same familial love and life force. Indeed, all through the serialization of *The Field Path*, the author seeks to restore the landscape of "home," a place where "everything, each and every object, gives off its own light" ("The Fragrant Well")—a seeking, in its turn, most likely fueled by his faith in the power of family and the original life force. He dreams of a "fragrant well" from which we might find, once more, that disappearing love of family, that original life force.

Lee Gyeong-ho

박범신

1946년 충남 논산 출생으로 전주교대를 거쳐 원광대 국문과와 고려대 교육대학원을 졸업했다. 1967년부터 1973년까지 초등학교와 중학교 교사 생활을 하였고, 1973년《중앙일보》신춘문예에 소설『여름의 잔해』가 당선되어 등단하였다.

김승희―정호승 등과 함께 '73그루프'를 조직하여 동인으로 활동하였다. 1978년 첫 창작집『토끼와 잠수함』을 낸 이래로『은교』(2010),『소금』(2013)에 이르기까지, 예닐곱 권의 창작집을 포함하여 사십여 편의 장편소설의 소설을 펴냈고, 현재에도 섬세한 묘사와 감각적 필치로 '영원한 청년작가'로서 왕성한 창작활동을 전개하고 있다.

『죽음보다 깊은 잠』(1979),『풀잎처럼 눕다』(1980) 등의 초기작이 출간 이후 베스트셀러가 되면서 1970~80년대 가장 대중적인 인기 작가 중 한 사람으로 활약한다. 1970~80년대의 작품들은 대체로 도시적 폭력의 구조적인 근원을 밝히면서, 거대한 폭력에 맞서는 주인

Park Bum-shin

Born in 1946 in Nonsan, Chungcheongnam-do, Park Bum-shin attended Jeonju National University of Education and studied Korean Literature at Wonkwang University before going on to the graduate school of education at Korea University. Park was working as an elementary and middle school teacher from 1967 to 1973, when he made his literary debut with "Summer Debris," which received an award in the *Joongang Daily*'s annual spring literary contest. Together with Kim Seung-hui and Jeong Ho-seung, Park helped found the "73 Group," an active literary circle of contemporaries. Between producing his first collection, *The Rabbit and The Submarine*, in 1978, and *Eungyo* (2010) and Salt (2013) in recent years, Park has written over forty novels and six or seven short story collections. Dubbed "eternally youthful" for his delicate descriptions and sensuous prose style, Park continues to be a productive and energetic presence in the contemporary literary scene.

After several of his early publications—*A Sleep*

공들의 도전과 좌절, 패배와 죽음의 결말을 그려낸다. 당시에 '대중 작가'라는 상업주의적인 명명 속에 비판의 대상이 되기도 했지만, 도시와 농촌(=고향)이라는 이분법적 대립구조를 통해 산업화 시대 이후 발생된 한국 사회의 타락한 인간형을 추적함으로써 이기주의적 인간세태와 폭력적 본성을 정밀하게 그려낸 작가로 평가받는다. 특히 이 시기 그의 문학은 감성적 묘사와 시적인 문체를 바탕으로, 비루한 삶과의 치열한 대결 의식, 도시 문명의 비정성과 이기주의적 인간 군상에 대한 비판 등을 다루고 있다. 그리하여 현대 도시인의 욕망과 좌절, 속물적 인간세태, 물질만능주의의 허상, 기회주의적 속성 등을 사실적이면서도 낭만적으로 형상화한다.

1993년 《문화일보》에 소설 『외등』을 연재하던 중 절필을 선언한 이후 삼 년 동안 칩거에 들어가 겸허한 자기 성찰의 시간을 갖게 된다. 삼 년 동안 진행된 성찰의 깊이와 사유의 내포는 1996년 《문학동네》 가을호에 중편소설 『흰소가 끄는 수레』 등을 발표하면서 표출된다. 이후 자전적 성찰이 담긴 연작소설집 『흰소가 끄는 수레』(1997)를 출간하고, 현재에 이르기까지 왕성한 필력으로 문학과 삶, 몸과 욕망, 자연과 생명에 관한 진지한

Deeper Than Death (1979), *Lie Like A Leaf* (1980)—became bestsellers, Park took on the mantle of one of the most popular writers of the 1970's and 1980's. Overall, Park's works from this period seek to lay bare the structural origins of urban violence, setting protagonists against large-scale organized crime operations while charting the progression of their defiance and frustration, often culminating in their death and defeat. Though, at the time, Park's christening as a popular author of "commercial fiction" made him the object of some criticism, even these older works are now appreciated for their detailed depictions of the violence of human nature and the egocentrism of contemporary society. This is especially true when set against the backdrop of Korea's increasing corruption in the wake of industrialization, all reflected through the binary structure of city/ country conflict (with the country here always represented as the perennial "home"). Indeed, it is particularly in these early works that Park applies his sensuous descriptions and poetic lyricism to the critical treatment of subjects like the egotism of the human masses, the cold-heartedness of urban civilization, and the conscious confrontation with the baseness of daily life. The desires and frustrations

탐색을 지속하고 있다.

작가가 성찰과 사유의 대상으로 선택한 공간은 히말라야이다. 에베레스트, 안나푸르나 등 히말라야를 십여 차례 다녀온 체험은 『나마스테』(2005) 등에 온전히 수록된다. 이후 2007년 9월부터 5개월 간 '네이버 블로그'에 연재한 이후 출간한 『촐라체』는 2005년 1월 히말라야 촐라체 봉(6440m)에서 조난당했다가 살아 돌아온 산악인 박정헌—최강식 씨의 이야기를 모티프로 삼고 있다. 작가 스스로 '갈망의 3부작'이라고 명명하면서, 『촐라체』는 히말라야를 배경으로 인간 의지의 수직적 한계를 다루고 있으며, 역사소설 『고산자』에서는 역사적 시간을 통한 꿈의 수평적인 정한(情恨)을 다루었고, 『은교』에 이르러 실존의 현실로 돌아와 존재의 내밀한 욕망과 그 근원을 탐험했다고 고백한다.

1995년부터 명지대학교 문예창작학과 교수를 지냈으며, 1981년 『겨울강, 하늬바람』으로 대한민국문학상(신인 부문), 2001년 소설집 『향기로운 우물 이야기』로 제4회 동리문학상, 2003년 『더러운 책상』으로 제18회 만해문학상, 2005년 『나마스테』로 한무숙문학상, 2009년 『고산자』로 제17회 대산문학상, 2010년 『은교』로 제

of the modern city-dweller; the shallowness of social conditions writ large; the illusory nature of materialism; the inner workings of opportunism: Park's works from this period manage to give form to all these issues and more while maintaining a balance between romance and realism.

In 1993, in the midst of serializing his latest work, *The Lamp*, in *The Munhwa Ilbo*, Park announced that he was giving up writing. For the following three years he lived in seclusion, devoting his time to humble introspection. The comprehensive reasoning behind this three-year period of reflection was eventually expressed in *The Cart Pulled By the White Cow*, a novella published in the 1996 winter edition of *Munhak Dongnae*. This reentry into the world of letters was soon followed by a collection of linked stories under the same title *The Cart Pulled By the White Cow*, published in 1997; since then, Park has continued to harness the considerable powers of his prose to explore literature, human life, the body, desire, nature, and existence itself.

As the primary setting of these more recent explorations, Park ultimately chose the space of the Himalayas. The story of his six treks to the Himalayas (including Mount Everest and Mount Annapurna) has

30회 올해의 최우수예술가상(문학 부문) 등을 수상했다.

been compiled in its entirety in his 2005 *Namasté*. His next major publication, *Cholatse* (originally serialized over five months on 'Naver Blogs' online, starting in September 2007), was about the near-loss and ultimate survival of mountaineers Park Jeong-heon and Choi Gang-sik on the Himalayan Peak Cholatse (6440m) in the January of 2005. The first part of what the author himself calls his 'trilogy on longing,' *Cholatse* is, in many ways, about the vertical limits of the human will. The second, a historical novel titled *Gosanja*, uses the lens of historical time to capture the horizontal nature of our inner worlds, while the third, *Eungyo*, attempts to explore the private desires—and the source of those desires—that follow a return to the realities of daily existence.

Park took a position as a professor of creative writing at Myongji University in 1995. He has received numerous awards, including the Republic of Korea Literary Award in 1981 for *Winter River, West Wind*, the Fourth Annual Dongri Literary Award in 2001 for *The Fragrant Well*, the Eighteenth Annual Manhae Literary Award in 2003 for Dirty Desk, the Han Moo-sook Literary Award in 2005 for *Namasté*, the Seventeenth Annual Daesan Literary Award in

2009 for *Gosanja*, and the Thirtieth Annual Artist of the Year Award (Fiction Category) in 2010 for *Eungyo*.

번역 **마야 웨스트** Translated by Maya West

리드 대학교를 졸업했고 2003년 한국 문학 번역원 신인상을 탔다. 현재 서울에 거주하며 프리랜서 작가, 번역가로 활동하고 있다.

Maya West, graduate of Reed College and recipient of the 2003 Korean Literature Translation Institute Grand Prize for New Translators, currently lives and works in Seoul as a freelance writer and translator.

감수 **전승희, 데이비드 윌리엄 홍**

Edited by Jeon Seung-hee and David William Hong

전승희는 서울대학교와 하버드대학교에서 영문학과 비교문학으로 박사 학위를 받았으며, 현재 하버드대학교 한국학 연구소의 연구원으로 재직하며 아시아 문예 계간지 《ASIA》 편집위원으로 활동 중이다. 현대 한국문학 및 세계문학을 다룬 논문을 다수 발표했으며, 바흐친의 『장편소설과 민중언어』, 제인 오스틴의 『오만과 편견』 등을 공역했다. 1988년 한국여성연구소의 창립과 《여성과 사회》의 창간에 참여했고, 2002년부터 보스턴 지역 피학대 여성을 위한 단체인 '트랜지션하우스' 운영에 참여해 왔다. 2006년 하버드대학교 한국학 연구소에서 '한국 현대사와 기억'을 주제로 한 워크숍을 주관했다.

Jeon Seung-hee is a member of the Editorial Board of ASIA, is a Fellow at the Korea Institute, Harvard University. She received a Ph.D. in English Literature from Seoul National University and a Ph.D. in Comparative Literature from Harvard University. She has presented and published numerous papers on modern Korean and world literature. She is also a co-translator of Mikhail Bakhtin's ***Novel and the People's Culture*** and Jane Austen's ***Pride and Prejudice***. She is a founding member of the Korean Women's Studies Institute and of the biannual Women's Studies' journal ***Women and Society*** (1988), and she has been working at 'Transition House,' the first and oldest shelter for battered women in New England. She organized a workshop entitled "The Politics of Memory in Modern Korea" at the Korea Institute, Harvard University, in 2006. She also served as an advising committee member for the Asia-Africa Literature Festival in 2007 and for the POSCO Asian Literature Forum in 2008.

데이비드 윌리엄 홍은 미국 일리노이주 시카고에서 태어났다. 일리노이대학교에서 영문학을, 뉴욕대학교에서 영어교육을 공부했다. 지난 2년간 서울에 거주하면서 처음으로 한국인과 아시아계 미국인 문학에 깊이 몰두할 기회를 가졌다. 현재 뉴욕에서 거주하며 강의와 저술 활동을 한다.

David William Hong was born in 1986 in Chicago, Illinois. He studied English Literature at the University of Illinois and English Education at New York University. For the past two years, he lived in Seoul, South Korea, where he was able to immerse himself in Korean and Asian-American literature for the first time. Currently, he lives in New York City, teaching and writing.

바이링궐 에디션 한국 대표 소설 038
향기로운 우물 이야기

2013년 10월 18일 초판 1쇄 인쇄 | 2013년 10월 25일 초판 1쇄 발행

지은이 박범신 | **옮긴이** 마야 웨스트 | **펴낸이** 방재석
감수 전승희, 데이비드 윌리엄 홍 | **기획** 정은경, 전성태, 이경재
편집 정수인, 이은혜 | **관리** 박신영 | **디자인** 이춘희
펴낸곳 아시아 | **출판등록** 2006년 1월 31일 제319-2006-4호
주소 서울특별시 동작구 흑석동 100-16
전화 02.821.5055 | **팩스** 02.821.5057 | **홈페이지** www.bookasia.org
ISBN 978-89-94006-94-9 (set) | 978-89-94006-01-7 (04810)
값은 뒤표지에 있습니다.

Bi-lingual Edition Modern Korean Literature 038
The Fragrant Well

Written by Park Bum-shin I **Translated by** Maya West
Published by Asia Publishers I 100-16 Heukseok-dong, Dongjak-gu, Seoul, Korea
Homepage Address www.bookasia.org I **Tel**. (822).821.5055 I **Fax**. (822).821.5057
First published in Korea by Asia Publishers 2013
ISBN 978-89-94006-94-9 (set) I 978-89-94006-01-7 (04810)